THE FLAT IN NOTTING HILL

Love and lust in the city that never sleeps!

Izzy, Tori and Poppy are living the London dream—
sharing a big flat in Notting Hill, they have good jobs,
wild nights out…and each other.

They couldn't be more different, but one thing is
for sure: when they start falling in love they're going
to be very glad they've got such good friends around
to help them survive the rollercoaster…!

THE MORNING AFTER THE NIGHT BEFORE
by Nikki Logan

SLEEPING WITH THE SOLDIER
by Charlotte Phillips

YOUR BED OR MINE?
by Joss Wood

ENEMIES WITH BENEFITS
by Louisa George

Don't miss this fabulous new continuity
from Modern Tempted™!

Dear Reader,

It was so much fun creating the world of *The Flat in Notting Hill* with my author friends Nikki Logan, Charlotte Phillips and Louisa George. E-mails frequently bounced between Australia, the UK, New Zealand and South Africa about the four linked books, and as we discussed the storyline we got to know each other a little better—that was a wonderful side-benefit of working with these lovely ladies. I'm sure our editors are quite glad that we live so far apart; I have no doubt that there would be a marked increase in ladies' lunches and a sharp decrease in productivity if we were closer!

Tori, my heroine, has really, really, *really* bad taste in men, and I had so much fun writing about her journey to love and acceptance. She's one of those heroines who wrote her own story; she kept surprising me and she frequently went off, did her own thing and left me scratching my head, muttering, 'That was *not* what I'd planned!' Matt, my hero, wasn't much better at following orders but, because I'm shallow, he'd just smile at me, flash me his abs, and I'd forgive him anything.

If you've picked this book up as a stand-alone, grab the other three books in the continuity and find out how the other flatmates got their happy-ever-after.

With, as always, my best wishes

Joss

PS Come and say hi via Facebook: Joss Wood Author, Twitter: @josswoodbooks or www.josswoodbooks.com

YOUR BED
OR MINE?

BY
JOSS WOOD

First published in Great Britain 2014
by Mills & Boon, an imprint of Harlequin (UK) Limited,
Eton House, 18-24 Paradise Road, Richmond, Surrey, TW9 1SR

© 2014 Harlequin Books S.A.

Special thanks and acknowledgement are given to Joss Wood
for her contribution to *The Flat in Notting Hill* series.

ISBN: 978-0-263-24313-0

Harleq
renewa
sustain   form
to the l

Printed
by CPI

Joss Wood wrote her first book at the age of eight and has never really stopped. Her passion for putting letters on a blank screen is matched only by her love of books and travelling—especially to the wild places of Southern Africa—and possibly by her hatred of ironing and making school lunches.

Fuelled by coffee, when she's not writing or being a hands-on mum Joss, with her background in business and marketing, works for a non-profit organisation to promote the local economic development and collective business interests of the area where she resides. Happily and chaotically surrounded by books, family and friends, she lives in Kwa-Zulu Natal, South Africa, with her husband, children and their many pets.

Other Modern Tempted™ titles by Joss Wood:

MORE THAN A FLING?
FLIRTING WITH THE FORBIDDEN
THE LAST GUY SHE SHOULD CALL
TOO MUCH OF A GOOD THING?
IF YOU CAN'T STAND THE HEAT…

This and other titles by Joss Wood are available in eBook format from www.millsandboon.co.uk

DEDICATION

To my son Rourke: gorgeous, smart and talented.

As you read this you'll be about to start an exciting new chapter in your life, but everyone knows that you'll be perfectly fine and that I'll be the basket case.

So as you head off I'd like you to remember to be bold, be funny, be *you*!

CHAPTER ONE

'UH-HUH...YEAH, BABY... Uh-huh...yeah, baybeeeeee...'

Oh, dammit, not porn, Tori Phillips thought, hearing the lusty moans as she closed the front door to Mark's apartment at the end of a hellish working day. Not at six-thirty on a Friday night when all she wanted was a cup of tea, her soft pyjamas and a silly reality show. She wanted to pull her hair up into a messy knot, eat ice cream out of the carton and be reassured that there were people in the world more screwed up than her.

Please, please, no porn—and, while she was asking, could they have a sex-free night too? She was too tired to play the leading role in Mark's Kama-Sutra-on-crack fantasies tonight.

'Mark?'

'In the bedroom.'

His voice, not deep at the best of times, always got a bit squeakier when he was excited and Tori twisted her lips in irritation. What was he watching, for goodness' sake? She looked longingly at the cold kettle as she passed through the kitchen.

'Uh-huh...yeah, baby... Uh-huh...yeah, baby...'

Definitely porn, Tori thought.

Damn. It.

That meant that Mark would be raring to go and she really, truly had a cracking headache. Barefoot in the passage of what was supposed to be her new home, Tori frowned, pushed open the door to the master bedroom and blinked. The TV on the wall was blank and the barnyard sounds came from the vicinity of the bed.

For a moment her brain couldn't process what she was seeing...another woman with pasty skin, heavy breasts and a rather large bum straddled her boyfriend and was riding him like a demented fairy. Fairy because she had the ugliest, dullest pair of wings tattooed across both butt cheeks. Tori expected her to take off in flight at any minute...

'Uh-huh...yeah, baby... Uh-huh...yeah...'

Dear Lord, Frantic Fairy came with a soundtrack. Four words, impressive...

Mark turned his head and caught her shocked look. He sent her a sly smile. 'Tori! It's about time you got home... we got tired of waiting so we decided to start without you. Get naked and Cinnamon will tell you what to do.'

Cinnamon? Seriously, that was her name? Tori shuddered and wished she could wash her eyes out with antibacterial soap.

'C'mon, Tori, get over here,' Mark wheedled, placing his rather small hands on those pendulous breasts. FF looked her up and down but didn't break her stride.

'Hey, honey, don't be shy. I'll be gentle.'

Uh...like, no, Tori thought, *a thousand nos.* Call her weird, but if girls didn't—even her in fantasies—turn her on then there was no chance of her getting it on with a skanky-looking girl with tattooed fairy wings on her butt.

So, apparently there were some things she wouldn't do for love. This was good to know.

'Get over here, Vicky...it'll be fun,' Mark ordered, pumping his hips.

'Don't call me Vicky...' Tori snapped. Like *that* was important right now. God. She glared at them both, tasting rage in the back of her throat. The urge to scream at them was overwhelming.

It took a lot of effort for her to keep her tone low and cool. 'Give me a sec, okay...*honey*?' She pasted a thin smile on her face. 'I'm just going to grab some things and you can carry on. A little warning, though...he's very quick off the trigger.'

The movement on the bed stilled as they both looked at her.

'Oh, God, you're going to be bitchy about this,' Mark said. Anyone would think she'd caught him drinking milk out of the carton, not screwing a peroxide blonde with inch dark roots.

'Maybe I should have run this by you before you came home...' Mark conceded.

Tori lifted an eyebrow. You think? She caught his hips lifting and thought that she might be sick. 'Are you really going to discuss this while you're still on the job?'

It was like watching the footage of a really huge natural disaster, horrific but fascinating, Tori thought as Mark patted FF's hip. She climbed off him and lay back on the rumpled bed, her long-suffering sigh audible from across the room. Mark sat up, his penis—his condom-covered penis...*thank God for small mercies!*—still ready to party.

So, apparently, he wasn't completely stupid...

And it was equally apparent, she thought as she eyed his still small but straight-as-an-arrow erection, that she was the only one who Mark couldn't get a hundred per cent hard for. After all the work she'd put into their sex life, that was possibly an even bigger slap in the face than the fact that she'd caught him doing another woman in their bed and expected her to join in.

Tori briefly closed her eyes before stalking past the bed to the huge walk-in closet, reaching for her overnight bag on the top shelf. She pulled it down and grabbed under-wear, some T-shirts and clothes for the weekend.

'What are you doing?' Mark asked as she walked back into the room and headed towards the en-suite bathroom. She flicked him a glance. He'd swung his legs over the side of the bed and was looking irritated.

'Making freaking cupcakes,' she snapped. 'What the hell do you think I'm doing?'

'You're overreacting, Vicky.'

Tori sent him a look that was designed to shrivel his balls. Damn, it didn't work. Tori walked in the bathroom and swept her make-up and toiletries from the marble-top counter into the designer toiletry bag she'd bought Mark for his birthday. Walking back into the bedroom, she shoved the toiletries into her bag, picked it up and slung it over her shoulder.

Mark reached for a robe, pulled it on and ran a hand through his blond hair. 'This is your fault, you know, you don't give me what I need.'

'You're so full of it. God, Mark, but...*what the hell*?'

'I told you that I like it often and I like it varied—'

'Your often is ridiculous and your varied is halfway to weird! And this—' she waved her hand towards the bed '—this is unforgivable! And, for your information, there is *nothing* wrong with missionary style on the odd occasion!'

'You don't love me enough.'

I don't love you at all. The thought popped into Tori's head and it surprised her. Didn't she? She'd thought she did but then shouldn't she be feeling a lot more devasta-tion along with her overload of disgust?

'You're acting like a psycho and freaking out for no reason,' Mark told her before yawning, not bothering to put a hand over his mouth.

'Yeah, you really are hurting the vibe,' Frantic Fairy solemnly agreed.

She had to get out of here before she killed someone. Seriously. Prison orange was *so* not her colour.

Tori narrowed her eyes in warning. 'Screw you. Actually...' Tori just looked at her lying on the bed—*their* bed, on the sheets she'd bought and paid for!—naked and checking the messages on her mobile '...just screw him.'

All she'd wanted was a cup of tea, Tori thought as she sat in the back of the taxi as it took her home. Home to Lancaster Road, to Poppy and Izzy.

Izzy might not be there, she reminded herself. Izzy was with Harry now, in love and so damn happy it sometimes hurt to watch them. But Poppy would be home...

She just needed to get home and she would feel better. They loved her, they always had, and right now she needed to be around people who did.

Love, her holy grail, her constant search. It didn't have to be perfect, or a ballad or a fairy tale. She didn't want a prince but she sure as hell would like to be someone's princess.

But obviously not Mark's any more.

'*You...*' Izzy's voice was loud in her head '*...are the ultimate bum magnet when it comes to men, Toz. You look around and choose the most screwed-up guy in the room.*'

Maybe she did but there was always the divine hope that this man could be the one who could love her; intensely, absolutely, for ever.

She was a master of wishful thinking.

She should've dumped Mark ages ago but she'd kept hoping that she could change him, that she'd wake up one day and he'd be...better. And, let's be honest here, she adored the fact that she was centre of his unwavering attention, of being constantly and *continuously* wanted. It wasn't the love she craved but it was *something*...

It was enough of a something for her to ignore the

naughty text messages she'd seen on his phone, the teenager who'd rocked up at the door a couple of weeks ago looking for Mark, not to mention his ex-girlfriend who constantly called. She suspected that he'd dipped his ink in any and all of their wells but she'd never found the—what was Alex's expression?—the smoking bullet. They'd fought about it—hell, they fought about everything!—and she'd justified staying with him by thinking that their emotional, loud, crazy see-saw of life was better than her being alone and loads better than the cold war she'd grown up in around her parents. Hot fights were always better than derisive comments, sarcasm, frosty insults tossed out with a contemptuous, sneering smile. She'd take loud and explosive over quiet and deadly any day.

At least with volatile you got some sort of warning and you could *attempt* to avoid or contain the emotional bloodshed.

Quiet but deadly…wasn't that the perfect way to describe her parents' formal union? She was quite sure that if she called it a marriage the gods of love would nail her with a lightning bolt.

Mark wasn't perfect, far from it, but neither was she. But at least they expressed their emotions…loudly and often. Maybe too often to be healthy. And maybe he hadn't been the poster-boy boyfriend but he was someone to wake up to, go to sleep with. Be with.

Except that his smokin' bullet turned out to be a freaking nuclear bomb, Tori thought as the taxi pulled up next to her old home, the top-floor flat of a converted fire station with Ignite, an Italian bistro and coffee shop, on the bottom floor.

Wiping her now wet eyes with her fingers, she hauled in her breath and climbed out of the taxi, yanking her overnight bag from the floor.

How was she going to spin it this time? she thought,

looking up to the window of Poppy's flat. Since she was a little girl, Poppy's home had been hers too, the place and person she ran to when life kicked her to the kerb.

Poppy and Izzy, her oldest friends and the people who loved her best. They'd welcome her back as they always did and then they'd settle in, waiting for the story…because there was always a story. For once she just wished that she had the guts to drop her guard and tell it as it was. That she felt battered and bruised and emotionally flattened. Sad and so damn scared that she'd never find what she needed, what she was really looking for.

Petrified that she would soon be thirty, then forty, fifty and kept around for her charm, her entertainment value, her pretty face but still, under it all, unloved, unvalued and, worst of all, unneeded.

'Seriously, she was riding him so fast that I thought that her wings were going to launch her off him…'

Tori was in her favourite chair in the eclectic, messy, colourful sitting room of the flat, her bare feet tucked up under her and a glass of red in her hand. Poppy was in the wingback chair opposite her and Izzy sat on the ottoman next to her. Both were doubled over, clutching their stomachs and laughing uproariously.

Yeah, good job, Tori, she thought wearily. You've pulled it off again.

'Oh, God, Tori, stop.' Izzy whimpered between snorts of laughter. 'Your love life should be serialised as a soap opera, hon.'

'And Mark? How did he act?' Poppy asked, wiping her tears away.

'He didn't even bat an eye, just turned and said, "Get naked, join in, and What's-Her-Skanky will show you what to do."'

Two mouths fell open, perfectly synchronised. 'And you didn't know about this?'

'Hell, no!' Tori made herself smile. 'If I had, I would've had a say in who to pick as contestant number three. But really, God—*her*? She looked like a walking mattress. Besides, women just don't do it for me.'

'You did kiss Melissa Butler.'

'I was thirteen, Poppy! And you dared me to!' Tori stared up at the ceiling.

Poppy sat up, leaned forward and sent Tori a searching look. It was her Poppy patented, sneaky you-talk-a-good-game-but-I-know-you-are-full-of-BS look. 'Are you really okay, Toz? You're acting like you couldn't give a damn but—'

Tori tossed her hair and dredged up a reassuring smile. 'I'm fine, I promise. Mark is welcome to dip his ink into her radioactive well.'

'Talking of, please tell me that he's clean and so are you.' Poppy—Dr Poppy now—asked, frowning. 'Maybe you should come in for a check-up, let me run some tests. Do a complete physical.'

She was stupid emotionally but she wasn't a complete idiot. 'Relax, Pops. We always used condoms, Doctor. No exceptions, ever.'

'Promise?'

'Promise.' Poppy let out a huge sigh of relief and Tori was grateful that she'd never, not once—despite Mark's bitching—deviated from that rule. And Mark could bitch for days.

'On another subject…I'm homeless and I need to move back in. Can I have my old room back?'

Poppy and Izzy exchanged a frantic, *oh-no* look that had her heart crashing to the floor. If she couldn't move back in then she didn't know that she could hold it together. The only place she could contemplate being was in this flat, with these people. Poppy looked agitated. 'The problem is that Alex and Lara are in your room and I've rented Izzy's room to Isaac—'

'But isn't he away?'

'Yes, but—'

'She can have the boxroom,' Izzy interjected, 'since I've moved in with Harry.'

Ick, the boxroom. Tiny, cramped, child-sized bed. Jeez, it wasn't even big enough to swing a fly. No cupboard space, a tiny window and you could hear every noise from the bathroom and its old, rusty pipes.

On the plus side it didn't have her despicable ex in it. Win.

'I'll take the boxroom.' Tori sighed. 'Though I think that, as my mates, either you or Alex should consider giving up your rooms because I've been traumatised for life. I'm considering bleaching my eyes and brain with acid.'

Poppy stood up, patted her shoulder and took her wine glass. 'Yeah, *you'd* think that. Here's an idea—while you're suffering in the boxroom, think about choosing a man a couple of steps up the evolutionary scale from pond scum next time, okay?'

'Yes, Mum,' Tori grumbled.

'Seriously, she was riding him so fast that I thought that her wings were going to launch her off him...'

Matt Cross held the front door to his new digs open and considered reversing back through it. He instantly recognised the tone and notes of girl talk and it wasn't something he wanted to interrupt by walking into the lounge. He supposed that this was something that he'd have to put up with, together with scented rooms, lingerie and a slew of empty wine glasses scattered throughout the house.

It had been a long time since he'd shared a flat with anyone. Sharing a house with Poppy and Alex would take some adjusting to, but at least his clients didn't know where he was and couldn't rock up on his doorstop at all hours of the day looking for reassurance or company.

His eyebrows lifted at the drawling, low-pitched voice that sounded as if it belonged on the other side of a phone-sex conversation. Matt, not wanting to give his presence away, left the door open and peeked through the doorway to the lounge and saw the perfect profile of a streaky-haired woman with mile-long legs.

Whoah! Sexy.

Matt dragged his eyes away to look from Poppy, his landlord, to Izzy, whom he'd met before. The knockout must be—geez, what was her name? Laurie? Laura?—the third of the three original flatmates he had yet to meet. Izzy was bent double, wheezing with laughter, and Poppy was wiping her eyes.

Her smile was negated by the fact that she was clutching the stem of her wine glass so hard that he thought it might break at any minute. Mmm, she didn't think her story was quite as funny as they did.

Now that was interesting.

Then she lifted her face and stared at the ceiling and he caught the sheen of tears in her eyes, her rapid blinking. Hello…she was seriously distressed. Matt's instinct was to head straight for her, to gather her up and to tell her it was okay to let those tears fall.

Weird, slightly scary, since he didn't even know the woman. He watched, fascinated as she rearranged her features so that she looked like any other carefree woman in her mid-to-late twenties with wide eyes and a wider smile.

Oh, she was an excellent faker.

'He didn't even bat an eye, just turned and said, "Get naked, join in and What's-Her-Skanky will show you what to do."' She carried on with her story.

Now he had the urge to rearrange some clown's face.

Matt turned and lifted his eyebrows when Alex, Poppy's brother and another inhabitant of the flat, stepped into the spacious hallway behind him.

'Women just don't do it for me.'

'You did kiss Melissa Butler.'

'I was thirteen, Poppy!' she howled. *'And you dared me to!'*

Alex lifted his eyebrow at Matt before looking through the crack of the door and wincing.

'What's Tori's story this time?' he asked in a low voice, also seemingly reluctant to walk into the lounge.

Tori... Matt tested the name on his tongue and found that he liked it. He rubbed his hand over his forehead.

'I just got here but, as far as I can tell, she got home and her partner had arranged a surprise for her,' Matt quietly replied as he dropped his laptop case to the floor next to the battered hall table.

'Tori loves surprises so what's the big deal?'

'The surprise was a threesome which I gather she didn't expect and certainly didn't agree to.'

Alex tossed out a curse. 'And, let me guess, Tori's pretending it's a joke. Classic Tori.' Alex shrugged out of his coat and Matt saw his fist clench, release and fist again as he struggled to control his reaction. 'I'd happily rearrange his face, the bastard.'

Interesting, Matt thought. He knew that Alex was with Lara and could see that the guy was crazy mad over her. So why the instinctive reaction to protect Tori? And why didn't he like it? 'So that's the third friend they are always talking about.'

'Mmm. She, Poppy and Izzy have shared this flat for years and years but Tori moved out a couple of months back. I'm in her old room and you're using the turret room—Izzy's old room.

'I warned her about Mark. God, why didn't the bloody

woman listen?' Alex muttered. Matt was beginning to think that none of her friends liked Tori's threesome-loving boyfriend. Alex peeked through the door and raised his eyebrows when he heard Tori laugh. 'She's taking it very well…knowing how melodramatic Tori can be, I expected her to be throwing glasses and, possibly, furniture.'

Matt shuddered at the thought. He was grateful that she wasn't; he had to deal with enough drama from his clients without coming home to a hysterical, furniture-throwing woman.

And he put up with a fair amount of drama from his sports-star clients. As their agent, looking after the business side of their sporting careers was easy, he could negotiate deals blindfolded, but playing the role of psychologist, older brother, agony aunt and best friend was emotionally draining. That was why he was renting this room in an eclectic flat on the fringes of Notting Hill for the duration of his stay in London. He loved his job but he had so much to do while he was over here that he didn't want, or need, his UK clients dropping in on him at odd hours of the night or day.

Having them calling him all the time was enough of a pain. He was pretty sure that he was getting a repetitive strain in his elbow from constantly holding his phone to his ear. He planned to have a mini-holiday from being their agony aunt, their solver of all problems. As for women… he was sort of avoiding them too since his last hook-up back in Cape Town turned out to be a mini-stalker, utterly determined to be the first Mrs Cross.

There had only ever been one Mrs Cross—his mum—and he had no intention of changing that.

Ever.

Alex reached for his coat and shrugged it back on. Grabbing Matt's coat off the hook, he slapped it against his chest and tipped his head.

'Tori is the type that when she walks into a room and she's happy, birds sing, mountains move and the lights grow brighter. When she's miserable, tsunamis form, lava churns and demons howl. She sounds reasonably together now but she can turn on a dime. Besides, do we really want to hear about their thoughts on our junk?'

'Really don't.' Matt nodded his agreement.

He was happy to leave, if only to give the distress-concealing, lava-churning beauty some space. The friends wouldn't be able to talk, or chew the heads off bats, or do whatever females did when their worlds got turned on their heads if a stranger was in the room.

'Let's go to Isaac's place and grab a beer,' Alex suggested. 'He's not there but what the hell?'

'Which bar? He has a couple.'

'Red. It's an easy tube ride. We'll sneak back in later when the coast is clear.'

That, Matt decided, resisting the impulse to take another peek at the woman who could launch tsunamis and make demons howl, was the best idea he'd heard all day.

As they clattered down the stairs Alex threw a conversational grenade over his shoulder, straight at Matt's head. 'By the way, I'll wipe the floor with your face if you mess with Tori.'

Matt nodded. Warning received.

CHAPTER TWO

TORI, LYING ON THE super uncomfortable, lumpy and thin single mattress in the cramped boxroom, looked at the flashing display of her mobile and ignored Mark's call.

What number call was that? Sixteen, seventeen? She placed her forearm over her eyes, feeling drained, exhausted and so, so empty. She'd acted her ass off earlier but she knew that her friends, especially Poppy, hadn't bought it. Some of it but not all; they were too perceptive for her own good. Sometimes she thought that Poppy and Iz laughed because, knowing her so very well, they knew that was the reaction she was most comfortable with, because she always handled hurt with humour.

Tori hiccupped a sob and couldn't believe that she was crying over a man...again. It was what she did, she thought, a pattern of behaviour that started in her childhood and she'd yet to break. She'd throw herself into a situation, looking for attention—love, affirmation—and when it ran out, sometimes in minutes, sometimes days, weeks, months, she'd be left feeling flattened and...less than.

She was so tired of feeling less than. But the reality was that she'd never been enough...not for her parents, not for her previous loser boyfriends, definitely not for Mark.

Tori rolled over onto her side and groaned as a particularly large lump dug into her ribcage. On the plus side, she didn't love Mark, hadn't been able to open herself up to him and reveal the chronically insecure woman below her flash surface. Maybe if she found a man she could do that with, someone she allowed to peek below the party-girl, flirty-girl surface, maybe that would be the man she could fall in love with, the man who would give her the love and attention and the stability that had always been beyond her reach.

Tori thumped her wafer-thin pillow and rolled over again. This bed was disgusting, the room small and cramped. When she and Poppy and Iz shared this flat—happy, happy days of laughter, girl chats and wild parties—Izzy had used this room to store her clothes and Poppy her medical tomes. This bed had been a place to throw stuff on, now it seemed to be a repository for the lost and strayed, first Izzy, then Lara, now her.

But everything was changing… The flat was like Love Central recently, with Izzy falling head over heels in love with Harry and Alex losing his heart to Lara.

But she'd rather be here, in this horrible bed in the ti-niest room in the house with friends who cared about her, than back at Mark's with or without his plus one. This flat, originally a fire station with its exposed red brickwork and crazy plumbing, was the place she felt most like…well, herself, and the people who lived within its thick walls were more family than her own flesh and blood. Espe-cially Poppy, who knew her in and out and roundabout.

But really, this bed…she'd never get to sleep.

'Isaac is away…' Poppy had said.

Isaac is away…mmm, gorgeous Isaac. If he were in residence she'd consider making a play for him; he would be a super excellent way to forget Mark. Tori bit her lip… except that there was a weird vibe between Poppy and Isaac, something that would have her hesitating if Isaac were around…

But, right now, the bed in the turret room directly above

her head was big and comfortable and, best of all, empty! She could, at the very least, get a good night's sleep, something she knew would be next to impossible in this coffin.

Her mobile buzzed again and Tori sighed at the display. For a minute she considered answering it, considered allowing Mark to talk her around, to persuade her to jump into a taxi and come home. She'd make him grovel and, after endless hours of discussion, she'd have a warm body to curl up around tonight...

No! She was not that pathetic, that weak! He'd crossed a line as big as the San Andreas fault line and it was not okay! She was worth more than that...

Mind made up, Tori switched off her mobile, slid out of bed and walked up the stairs to the turret room, avoiding the stairs that creaked and the floorboards that groaned. In the morning, she thought as she opened the door to Izzy's old room, she would feel better, calmer, and more able to make rational decisions.

Maybe. Or maybe she'd cave and go back to Mark...

'You're sounding stronger, Dad.' Matt leaned back against the headboard, mobile to his ear.

'I'm fine. Don't worry.'

Matt twisted his lips at Patrick's sharp retort. Like him, he hated being fussed over, but Matt wasn't convinced that his dad was fully recovered from the bout of pneumonia that had hospitalised him at the beginning of August. He still sounded weak, although he tried to hide it.

And also like him, his father was a night owl and they often spent time on the phone between the hours of eleven and one in the morning. They'd chat about sport or the news and every so often Matt would explain a complicated deal he was involved in. Despite his years spent working in non-profit organisations promoting sport amongst disadvantaged children, Patrick had never lost his cool, unemotional, law-trained mind and his insights were frequently sharp, concise and devastatingly accurate. He had a way of cutting through the waffle and discarding the emotion to reveal the heart of the problem, the soul of the dilemma.

'How's Angela?' Matt asked, referring to the woman his dad had met a couple of months ago.

'Fine but she's not your mother.'

'No one is, no one could be,' Matt said gently, as he had a hundred times before. And as always he was instantly transported back to those awful months after her death, his dad sobbing at night, grief racking his body when he thought Matt was asleep. How many nights had he been woken by that low keening? How many times had he slipped out of his bed to lie in the passageway next to his dad's closed door, listening until his father finally stopped crying and drifted off to sleep?

'Twenty-two years, Matt, and I'm still as in love with her as I was. They say that people forget their loved ones, that they don't remember their faces, their voices. I still remember everything. Her wide green eyes, her raucous laugh, the way she always stuck her tongue between her lips when she was concentrating.'

And because his dad remembered so much, and spoke of her often, he did too. He'd adored his mother, grieved her death, but her passing had also taught him that marriage and love equated to heart-wrenching grief and he'd decided, at the ripe old age of eleven, to have nothing to do with it.

They were getting morbid, Matt thought, and changed the subject. 'So, I think I have a new flatmate...'

Matt explained the circumstances around Tori's arrival and soon Patrick was chortling in amusement. His dad wasn't a prude, thank God. He could talk to him about anything and he did.

'Oh, and I went to see your uncle Alfred yesterday.'

Matt tuned out as Patrick updated him on the health of his great-uncle and just listened to the comforting hum of his dad's voice. After his mum died, they'd stumbled through their lives. Patrick had learned to cook and to listen; mopped up spilt milk, broken windows from cricket balls and Matt's own childhood tears. Cricket had turned to rugby, and excruciating lectures about sex and girls had been suffered through—by both of them—and they'd both had to wrap their heads around his dad dating again. But Patrick had kept his sex life away from him—thank the Lord—and nothing and no one had disturbed their masculine, sports-crazy home.

It had been a blow to realise that, while he was good at cricket and great at rugby, he wasn't good or great enough. He was an excellent sportsman but just wasn't brilliant… he didn't have enough raw talent to take his sport to the next level. But that didn't mean that he couldn't work in the field, Patrick had constantly reminded him. He could always be associated with sport…

And now Matt represented twenty of the biggest names in sport that he personally looked after and his two associates had another sixty they represented between them. One of his tasks while he was in London was to consider hiring a UK-based agent to expand his business.

Matt heard a noise on the landing outside and glanced at the luminous hands on his sports watch. It was long past midnight and he wondered who else was up.

'Dad, sorry, I've got to go. Speak soon and look after that chest!'

He tossed his mobile onto the side table, sat up and rested his elbows on his knees. His eyebrows lifted when his door handle dipped and the door slowly opened. He'd always had excellent night vision and didn't need light to discern the slight female form, perfectly curved. As she turned to close the door her slithery robe rustled and he was treated to the most luscious bottom he'd seen in a very long time. Her hair was streaked and her profile, caught in the landing light just before she shut the door, showed a small, straight nose, full lips, deep-set eyes and a round, stubborn chin.

She stopped by the far side of the bed and he watched as small hands went to the belt on her robe and the fabric slipped off her shoulders revealing perky breasts, a flat stomach, slim hips and those fabulously long and silky legs.

Birds sang, and an orchestra started playing and he was quite sure that a mountain, somewhere in the world, moved. She was that sexy, he thought, as lust shot straight to his groin and belted up his spine.

Ah, the actress from earlier.

Which raised the question: what the hell was she doing in his room?

Naked?

Ooh, Tori thought, wiggling under the covers, a nice firm, lump-free bed. High thread count, clean cotton sheets, a decent feather pillow. Thank you, Isaac, for being in Amsterdam or Paris or somewhere else exotic doing cocktail-bar stuff and leaving your room empty for me to borrow. She sighed happily. This was a million times better; she could get a decent night's sleep in this comfy bed and she'd feel so much better in the morning: stronger, bolder, better able to cope. She rolled over on her side and dropped her hand to the mattress...

Except that wasn't a mattress. Tori froze. It was warm and hairy and the muscles underneath her hand contracted and released.

She'd known enough male bodies to immediately realise that she was holding a very muscular male thigh and because she could feel something that felt like a testicle brushing her pinkie finger, she suspected that her hand had landed quite far up his thigh—far as in 'far too close'.

Okay, she really hadn't planned on feeling Isaac up this evening. And why did she immediately feel guilty? Because of Poppy, she realised. Poppy and Isaac had something cooking; what it was she wasn't sure but it was *something*...

And while she had many, many, many faults, stealing her best friend's man—potential man—wasn't one of them.

If she was desperately lucky, then Isaac would be asleep and she could sneak back out and keep her mouth shut for ever and ever and ever...

Tori, trying to be very stealthy, lifted her thumb off his thigh, then her index finger, middle and ring finger and finally her pinkie. Pulling her hand away, she sighed with relief when there was no reaction from the body and slowly started to inch her way out of the bed.

A deep, sexy-as-sin voice growled at her through the darkness and pinned her to the bed. 'Where are you going? It was just starting to get interesting.'

'Isaac?' she whispered and held her breath, desperately hoping that Isaac had acquired a slight accent she didn't remember him ever having.

'Nope. Sorry.'

Sometimes, Tori thought, you are the statue and sometimes you are the pigeon. Obviously her day to be the statue wasn't quite over just yet.

The bedside light snapped on at the same moment that Tori bailed out of bed, the hounds of embarrassment snapping on her heels. She was halfway around the bed and still eight feet from where she dropped her robe—serve her right for being a slob and just dropping clothes on the floor—when she realised that he could see her in all her naked, jiggling glory!

'Eeep!' She instinctively slammed her forearm against

her boobs, cupped her pubic strip with her hand and stood there with her mouth hanging open, a deep red flush covering every inch of her body.

Help, help, help, help, help...

What to do...? What to do...? What to do...?

Seeing the corner of the loose duvet draped over the corner of the bed, she yanked it up and bailed underneath it, only taking another breath when she knew that every inch of her body was covered. Of course, she could still feel the long, long length of him—they were only separated by the sheet—but at least he couldn't see her!

Dear Lord, who was he? She was going to kill Poppy, slowly and with an evil smile on her face.

Tori felt fresh air slide in under the duvet and knew that he'd lifted it up to look at her. She turned her face into the mattress and gnawed the bottom of her lip.

'Hey there...'

Ooh, he had the nicest voice. Deep, mellow, like an aged whisky on a freezing winter's night.

'Want to come out from under there so that I'm not talking to your—admittedly gorgeous—tortoiseshell head?'

Tortoiseshell? Say what? Tori frowned while her brain turned over his words. Huh, he must mean her hair and the various shades of colour. Browns, reds, blondes...tortoiseshell. Dave, her hairdresser, would love that description.

Okay, so not the point.

Tori pulled her face out of the mattress, breathed deep and lifted her eyes and found herself looking up at a bigger, broader and—obviously—hairier chest than hers. He had just the right amount, she thought, a perfect black T that dusted his pecs and drifted into a luscious line that flowed over a stone-hard A-pack. The sheet covered his hips and she managed to contain her sigh of disappointment. Her eyes ambled upward again, noticing a crescent-shaped scar on his lower rib, the flat masculine nipples, muscled shoulders, thick arms, an angular jaw covered in black stubble, a wide mouth tipped up in amusement and eyes the colour of...

'British racing green,' she murmured, the words sliding out of her mouth.

'Excuse me?'

She wanted to wave her hand but instead she held the duvet to her chest. 'Your eyes, they are the exact shade known as British racing green,' she said, blushing and ducking her head into the mattress again. She sounded like such a twit; she'd snuck into his bed—naked—and she was wittering on about his eyes.

They were beautiful but...really?

Oh, fudge. Her face flared and she hoped he didn't notice. There was only one way to get out of this situation and that was to brazen her way through it. She wasn't in PR for nothing, she decided, and had plenty of practice.

Taking all her courage in both hands, Tori kept the duvet firmly in place and wiggled her way up so that she was sitting upright, the duvet tucked under her arms.

'Hello,' he said, his mobile mouth quirking up in a half-smile.

'Um...hi.' Tori pushed her hair out of her face and straightened her shoulders. 'Sorry about this.'

'I got to see a gorgeous naked girl. No need to apologise.'

Ignoring the flare of heat that she knew was still staining her cheekbones, Tori pushed her hand through her hair and smiled her patented I'm-a-girl-of-the-world smile. He didn't need to know that she was feeling anything but and her spirit was, well, not broken...cracked, dented, bruised? Bruised. That was the perfect word for how she was feeling...along with battered, drained and a healthy dose of smarting.

But since she had many years of practice of hiding her

feelings she just kept that stupid smile on her face and carried on bluffing. 'So, I guess the question is, who are you and what are you doing in Iz's bed?'

'Matt Cross and I'm renting the room for the month while Isaac is away. And that raises the question, what are you doing in Izzy's, Isaac's, temporarily my bed?'

'I heard there was a good-looking guy in it and thought I'd check you out.' Tori regretted the words before they even left her mouth.

'If that was true then you wouldn't have spent the first five minutes burrowing under the covers whimpering with embarrassment,' Matt calmly stated.

So the guy wasn't afraid to call BS. Good to know.

'So, give me another explanation,' Matt asked, after bunching up a pillow and placing it between his head and Iz's iron headboard.

'I've just had a really bad day and I wanted a decent night's sleep. The bed in the boxroom is a torture device and I knew that Isaac was away so here I am.'

'Here you are,' Matt agreed. 'So, I'm presuming you're Tori of the bad boyfriend and the Frantic Fairy story of earlier?'

'How on earth do you know about that?' Tori demanded.

'I was in the hall when you were concocting the story for Izzy and Poppy. That has got to hurt like hell.'

Concocting? That was an interesting, very truthful, turn of phrase. Tori cursed silently and bit her lip. She was sitting in bed, naked, with the hottest man she'd—literally—stumbled across in her life and he knew that her boyfriend had brought home another woman for a threesome. And he was sympathising with her...

Could this evening, possibly, get any worse? 'Oh, I was about to kick him into touch anyway so I don't really care,' she said, lying her head off. She did not need his sympathy or, worse, his pity. God.

'You have piggy eyes from crying. And your words and body are stiff with tension. Oh, yeah, you talk a good game but it hurts. How can it not?'

Tori sighed. She was not one of those women who cried well… She didn't have gentle tears that rolled out in perfect droplets and didn't wreck her make-up. She gushed and she was obviously violently allergic to her own tears because her eyes swelled up and turned blood red, her face blotched and Rudolf envied her nose. As a result, she generally avoided meeting flame-hot men until she looked normal again. No wonder Green Eyes was looking at her as if she were an alien species…not generally the reaction she normally got when she found herself naked in a man's bed. She'd never been particularly vain but she knew that men generally found her attractive. It was mortifying to be the object of pity, of concern, of *zero sexual interest*.

Focus, Tori, and start thinking of a way that you can get out of here with your dignity and pride intact. Actually, she'd settle for just getting *out*; pride and dignity were on their own.

I could seduce him…

Whoa, whoa, what? The words popped into her head and her eyes widened. Bad, bad idea, terrible idea, are you nuts?

He's a good-looking guy…

He's every gorgeous male celebrity wrapped up in one delicious package but that doesn't mean that you should make a play for him. You're upset, feeling emotionally beaten up and you never make good decisions when you're in this frame of mind…so keep your big mouth shut! Dear God, you are a basket case, Phillips.

Great sex—he looked the type who knew what he was doing in the sack—and a soft bed, a body to curl up around afterwards…

'Down, Tiger.' That dark-chocolate voice broke into her

chaotic thoughts and she bristled at the undisguised amusement she saw in his eyes, in the tilt of that sexy mouth.

'Excuse me?'

'That mind of yours is working the angles; flipping through your options.'

Tori licked her lips and looked for and found her coolest expression. 'I have no idea what you're talking about.'

'You know exactly what I'm talking about,' he drawled. 'But, okay, let's spell it out…you're running through scenarios; you're not happy that I know that you had a horrid experience at the hands of a man who, frankly, needs someone to teach him how to treat a woman. I'd be happy to oblige. You're also telling yourself that you don't want to go back to that bed or, if you were honest, admitting that you don't want to be alone.'

He'd be happy to beat Mark up for her? Now there was an idea…concentrate Tori! As nice as his statement made her feel, he was still looking past her breeziness to the truth below and she didn't like it and she wanted him to stop. She scowled at him. 'Nonsense.'

'Honey, if you weren't scared of being on your own you wouldn't still be in this bed, you would've hightailed it out of here the minute you realised you made a mistake. Instead, you're lying there looking like a wet dream thinking about making a play for me, thinking about whether you could seduce me or not.'

Dammit, this guy was perceptive.

'You probably could; I'm a man and you're…' his eyes flicked up and down her body '…you're seriously hot.'

Dark blue eyes collided with green and that lightning rod of attraction arced between them. Tori could see herself writhing over that body, her hair trailing along his chest, across his stomach. As if he knew what she was thinking, his Mr Get It On tented the bedclothes. Oh…oh, wow.

'You need to stop looking at me like that or else you're

going to be flat on your back in ten seconds and I'm not going to able to stop what comes next.' Matt growled. Tori pulled her eyes back up to his and saw that his gaze could melt her panties…if she were wearing any. Dear Lord, if she scooted over just a bit she could have those big hands on her body, that mouth on hers…

'You're killing me, woman,' Matt muttered, his thumb lifting to press her bottom lip. 'But sleeping with me isn't the antidote for whatever happened tonight.'

Tori swallowed and looked at her hands. 'I told you, I was about to kick him into touch anyway.'

'No, you weren't. You know it and I know it,' Matt said, his voice gentle. God, she could cope with attraction and lust and flirting but she couldn't cope with this stunningly attractive man looking past her brave girl façade and seeing the mess she was inside.

Matt leaned sideways, dropped his arm and when he straightened again, he clutched a navy T-shirt in his fist. Shaking it out, he draped the hole over her head and the big shirt fell over her chest. She slipped her arms into the shirt and allowed the duvet to drop. She hauled in the masculine scent of his deodorant and aftershave and that essence of masculinity that made her girly stuff hum. 'Thanks.'

Matt grunted, shoved the covers off and in one fluid movement stood up and stalked naked across the room. Tori's eyes followed the most excellent back and butt and long, muscled legs to the chest of drawers and sighed with frustration when he yanked out a pair of sweatpants and covered all that lusciousness up. Damn, damn, damn…she wasn't finished perving yet. Then Matt grabbed another T-shirt and pulled it on.

She thought she heard him mutter something about being a saint and stupid before he turned back and resumed his place next to her on the bed. He sat up so that his back was against the headboard and crossed his legs at the ankles.

Serious eyes met hers and Tori licked her lips at the compassion she saw within them. Then she yelped when he leaned forward, snuck an arm around her waist and hauled her up to him. His big hand forced her head onto his shoulder and his other hand rested on her lower back.

Tori lay in his embrace, her body radiating tension. What did this mean? Was he actually going to try and seduce her after all? And if he was, where was the kissing, the touching? Instead, Matt just switched off the light and they lay in the darkness and Tori felt his chest rise and fall beneath her cheek, heard the solid, reassuring thump-thump of his heart.

Inexplicably, tears started to build again and before she could stop them, they rolled down her face and dropped onto the material of his shirt. Matt's hand tensed and relaxed on her back and then he patted the top of her butt. That little tap was like the secret code that opened the gates to waterworks hell and her tears started to fall, thick and fast.

Matt didn't say anything, but just held her and allowed her to cry. Silent, long, scary tears that didn't seem to want to stop…tears that sucked her energy out of her, making her feel bone-deep tired. She closed her eyes against the burning sensation and it felt so good that she just kept them closed.

Tori sniffed, thought about lifting her head off his chest, decided she was too comfortable and stayed where she was. 'Aren't you going to tell me that it will get better and that worse things in the world happen to good people every day?' she asked. 'Aren't those the platitudes people dish out at times like these?'

'It will get better and worse things do happen but that's not what you need to hear right now.'

Tori looked up at him, his profile strong in the room full of shadows. 'What do I need to hear?'

'You need to hear that it hurts because it matters, that he treated you badly and that was wrong. You have a right to cry, to feel sad, to feel used.' Matt stroked her hair. 'You are allowed to feel miserable and you are allowed to show people that you feel miserable.'

Tori turned his words over in her mind, knowing that there was a fundamental truth within them but not able to grasp it, believe it. It was as if it were a finger of fog drifting past and her fingers kept sliding through it. Eventually she gave up trying to capture that nugget of truth and just listened to the thump-thump of Matt's heart.

Tori had no idea when she fell asleep...just that she did and it felt good and right. For the first time in a long time, in a stranger's arms, she felt safe.

Accepted. Enough.

Feeling as if she could just be...

CHAPTER THREE

TORI WOKE UP with a massive erection pushing into her lower back and she sighed with pleasure. Keeping her eyes closed, she stretched and wiggled her butt into that thick, hard long length of him. The hand on her breast tightened in response and a masculine thumb flicked over her nipple, pulling it into a hard peak, the cotton fabric adding to the pleasure.

Cotton fabric, T-shirt…Matt's T-shirt. Dear God, she was in bed with Matt, the sexy stranger from last night who'd held her, for the longest time, while she'd cried.

She'd cried? God, no.

She could cope with people thinking she was a diva, a bitch, a crazoid, but fragile? No bloody way! Dammit, she seldom cried and she never, ever, ever cried in front of anyone, she thought as her body tightened with tension. She'd never felt safe enough, especially not as a child, and that habit had carried over into her adult life. No, it was a lot easier, safer to put a smile on her face and fire off a joke…

She couldn't believe that she had blubbed all over Matt, all over a stranger! She'd had a couple of one-night stands over the years but the walk of shame was nothing to how mortified she felt right now; this was like doing the walk of shame naked, across broken glass and hot coals.

He must think she was weak and helpless and…wimpy.

She was Tori Phillips and she didn't do wimpy…and

there was no way that she could let this man, this gorgeous, sexy über-masculine man think that she was delicate, help-less...vulnerable. She wasn't any of those things...and, if she was, she didn't want him realising that she was.

She'd prefer to poke her eye out with a hot stick.

'Bad idea, Cross,' she thought she heard him mutter as his hand left her breast. Tori felt him kiss the top of her head; it was a placating, gentle, *there-there* kiss and it raised every hackle she had. She didn't need his pity or his sympathy...and she'd make damn sure that when he thought of her he wouldn't think of the snivelling, pathetic creature that had fallen asleep in his arms.

And there was only one way she knew of that would burn that image out of his head...

Sitting up, she whipped the T-shirt over her head and swung her leg over his hips and straddled him, her feminine core pressed into his erection. Tori cursed the fabric of his sweatpants and wished she'd yanked them down before positioning herself. Now she'd have to get off him, pull his pants down...

Matt's huge hands on her hips kept her from wiggling and he looked up into that part-angel, part-devil face and sighed. Her eyes radiated determination but he could still see mortification lingering there. Yep, there was too much of her brain involved in this decision. She wanted him, it seemed that they were instantaneously, fiercely attracted to each other, but there was something else in her eyes, in her expression that hinted at an emotion other than 'let me lick you from top to toe'.

'What are you doing, Tori?'

Tori lifted her perfectly arched eyebrow and sent him a naughty smile as her hands skimmed over his stomach. Pity her eyes didn't echo it. She wiggled against him and he couldn't help pushing up into her. Damn, she felt hot and wet and so amazingly wonderful.

'You seem bright enough, you figure it out.' Tori leaned forward and nibbled his bottom lip with her teeth. His tongue shot out to taste her mouth and he pulled it back at the last minute. If he kissed her, if he moved his hands off her hips, he wouldn't be able to stop rolling her over and plunging inside her.

She was perfect: long neck, slim shoulders, perky breasts that filled his hands and topped with blush pink, ultra-responsive nipples. A flat, flat stomach and a meticulously groomed strip of light brown hair that hinted at her natural colour. And the heat and moisture between her legs suggested warm, wet honey...

'This isn't a good idea.' he muttered against her lips. It so is, Mr Long and Strong protested. 'Not. A. Good. Idea.'

'You saying no?' Tori teased, her pointed tongue licking the dent in his cheek that his mum used to call a dimple but he called a pain-in-his-shaving-ass.

Was he saying no? Well, he was trying to... He had no moral objection to making love to a gorgeous woman but he wasn't sure of her motives, of why she was doing this. If it was only about pure sex he'd be all over her like a rash but he could still feel the tension in her, could see the flickers of emotion in her eyes that told him that there was a whole bunch of this puzzle he was missing.

He knew what pure lust looked like and there was nothing like it in her eyes. Mortification, determination, a little crazy maybe...pure lust, not so much.

Matt didn't like puzzles and he didn't like uncertainty and false motives.

'I'm saying no.' They were the hardest words he'd ever said but he forced them between his teeth, made his lips spit them out. Tori sat up slowly, her face utterly confused.

'What?'

Matt gripped her hips, bunched his muscles and with a grunt lifted her off him and onto the mattress next to him. He rolled his legs out of the bed, stood up and walked towards the door and scooped up her dressing gown, which he threw in her direction.

His mobile chirruped that he had a message and he glanced at the screen. A client, of course. He ignored the message, thinking that he should deal with one problem at a time.

'You're saying no?' Tori demanded.

Matt winced.

It wasn't even seven o'clock and he needed an aspirin. Actually he needed sex but since he'd just shot that in the foot, he'd settle for aspirin. His mobile chirped that he had another message.

'What the hell is wrong with you?' Tori demanded, finally pulling on her dressing gown and covering up that take-me-now body. Long and Strong sighed and began to settle down. Thank God for small, or, in his case, not so small mercies.

Matt kept his voice calm. 'Look, I just don't think it's a good idea… It's never a good idea to nail someone else just after you were dumped.'

'I wasn't dumped!' Tori's face scrunched up in fury as she scrambled out of his bed. 'I left him!'

'Whatever. And you're in someone else's bed not twelve hours later. You're vulnerable and sad and it's a recipe for a disaster.'

'It was a recipe for a mutual orgasm!' Tori howled. 'What are you, the male equivalent of a prick tease?'

Whoah, that wasn't fair. His eyes narrowed in warning. 'I never led you on—you were the one crawling all over me. Look, Tori, we're going to be living in the same flat for the foreseeable future…and all we're going to do is complicate the situation. Alex will rip my head off if I sleep with you when you are feeling vulnerable and hurt and I'm just a rebound screw for you.'

'I am *no*t vulnerable. I am fine,' Tori said through gritted teeth.

He didn't believe her and wanted to call her on it, but thought he'd just inflame the situation more. Instead he just motioned to the door. 'Why don't you get going before the rest of the flat gets wind of this...if they haven't already?'

'I don't care if—'

'You should,' Matt interrupted. 'You should care what the people who love you think.'

Tori tightened the sash of her dressing gown and pushed her messy hair away from her face. Her chin lifted as she gave him a look that was meant to eviscerate all his internal organs. 'You'll regret this.'

Matt scrubbed his face with his hands and then placed them on his hips. He watched as Tori stalked over to the bedroom door, yanked it open and slammed it so hard that the entire building shook. Well, if their flatmates weren't awake yet they would be now...

Matt crossed over to the window, yanked the sash window up, placed his hands on the sill and breathed in the chilly morning air. It was a good substitute for a cold shower and he felt himself shrink to everyday proportions. He'd done the right thing, he assured himself. He didn't need any complications in his life—and Tori had complications graffitied all over her in DayGlo spray paint—and sleeping with his brand-new flatmate would cause complications he didn't need.

He especially didn't need the protective Alex beating the snot out of him for taking advantage of her.

Okay, so...interesting start to his month in London.

She wasn't his type? Seriously?

His words reverberated around her brain as Tori sat at

the kitchen table later that morning, scowling into the mug of coffee cradled in her hands. How could he say that when she had the proof that she was exactly his type pressed hot and flush and throbbing against her, begging to slide on in?

Not her type? She was old enough to know that men thought that any naked woman floated their boat.

As God was her witness he was so going to regret those words. It was the second time she'd been verbally, emotionally slapped by a man in two days and she was sick of it. She was Tori Phillips, the life and soul of any party, champion flirt; she made people laugh and people liked her, dammit. Men *loved* her...

And he would too. Tori narrowed her bright blue eyes, deep in thought. Her pride demanded that she take some sort of action to bring him down a peg or two—or sixty thousand—and she was just the girl to show him the error of his ways. She tapped her French-manicured nail against her coffee mug; she could unleash the full power of her charm on him and when she had him at her feet and begging, she'd watch him squirm as she walked away.

Poppy might be smart, Iz ambitious but, by God, she was the most charming and, undoubtedly, the most stubborn and...and...and unforgiving of the bunch.

And, also the most screwed up of all of them. Why couldn't she just shrug off his words and let it go? Was she that insecure, that crazy? Yeah, she was. She wasn't book smart like Poppy, who was her stable rock, calm and in control. She wasn't like Iz, ambitious and driven. Iz had recently given up her high-flying career to work as a fund-raiser for charities, she had found Harry and was deliciously happy, but she knew what she wanted and how to get it.

No, Tori was the clown of the group, the emotional firecracker, the one they worried about, talked about and tried to keep grounded. She was capricious—she worked in PR, could anything be more flighty than that?—and she was emotional and high-maintenance. Or so they kept telling her.

Her friends loved her, dearly, but she knew they despaired of her. She knew that they desperately wanted to say 'I told you so' about Mark. Poppy, the mother hen, wanted to scoop her up and wrap her in cotton wool.

She would be fine… She'd pick herself up and dust herself down.

Tori smelt Poppy's scent before she even heard her and sighed with pleasure when Poppy's slim arms wrapped around her chest from behind. Poppy rested her temple against hers while Tori held her arms. Her best friend, her oldest friend. It was so good to be home…

'You okay, Toz?'

'I'm fine,' Tori replied as Poppy let her go. She looked up into Poppy's doubtful face. 'I'm fine, Popsicle. I promise. I'm bruised, not heartbroken. I'm considering sending Mark a thank you note…something along the lines of "thanks for waiting until I'd spent so much time with you and done so much with you to show me that you are, actually, a sex-addict sociopath".'

Poppy smiled. 'We knew that already.'

'Thanks for the warning,' Tori grumbled.

'You wouldn't have listened to it,' Poppy replied.

Tori waved her hand in the air. 'It doesn't matter—all men suck.'

Poppy put the kettle on the gas and shook her head. 'When are you going to start making better choices when it comes to men, Tori?'

'I have no idea,' Tori replied honestly.

Poppy shoved a tea bag into her mug and poured water on top. She prodded the bag with her finger and Tori winced, resisting the urge to hand her a spoon. Poppy lifted her amazing eyes and Tori saw that they were filled with worry…again. 'Something has got to change, Tori.'

'I know. I'm sorry.' Tori pushed her cup away. 'I should've listened to you…'

'Will you listen to me now?' Poppy leaned against the counter and sipped her tea while she waited for her response.

'Maybe.' She wished she could say yes but she didn't want to promise Poppy anything she couldn't deliver. She took her promises seriously.

'Take some time before you hurtle into the next crazy relationship. Stop confusing sex with love… Have sex if you have to but stop looking for love and investing in the man too soon. And you have to start choosing men who aren't complete idiots, Toz. You can't shake the asshat tree and expect a good man to fall out.'

Did she do that? Did she fall too hard and too fast, getting all her hopes up on something she deep down knew wouldn't last? Did she deliberately choose men who she knew were going to disappoint her? Hurt her? Was she a self-fulfilling prophecy?

Tori dredged up a smile. 'I hereby hand over my right to pick my own boyfriend because I obviously don't know what I am doing.'

'I'd do a happy dance if I actually believed that,' Poppy retorted. 'I just wish your heart would learn that it doesn't have to get involved in every situation. Its job is to pump blood, that's it.'

Tori, thinking that they'd spent far too much time talking about her obviously ridiculous love life, nodded at Poppy's white coat. 'Are you working today?'

Poppy grimaced. 'Yeah, sorry. How was your night in the boxroom?'

Interesting. Tori wrinkled her nose. 'Horrible. I want my room back!'

'I know and I'm sorry. But hang in there—Lara and Alex have been talking about taking a holiday soon, they want some sun…and some alone time, I suspect. When they go you can temporarily move back into your, their, room. And Isaac is away, by the way.'

Yeah, well, she'd found that out the hard way! Tori heard the twitch in Poppy's voice and her antennae picked up. She might be the one who was always in a crisis of one sort or the other and she did have a…ahem, colourful romantic history but she was emotionally intuitive and had always wondered why Poppy was so anti-relationships. They could talk about everything and did, except Poppy's personal life, which was a no-go, never-discuss area. Poppy, fun and self-effacing, was so universally adored that it was sometimes hard to remember that she hadn't ever—that Tori could remember—brought a man home…

But whenever Isaac's name was mentioned, whenever Isaac was around, Poppy vibrated with an energy that was weird and, if she wasn't mistaken, sexual. Isaac pushed Poppy's buttons and Tori was just glad that someone did.

'Oh, and Isaac offered his room for the month to Matt Cross, an old friend of his.' Poppy glanced at her watch. 'I've got to go; introduce yourself to Matt when you see him.'

She had. Matt had seen *all* of her.

Poppy banged her cup into the sink, whirled around and cupped Tori's face in her cool hands. 'I love you and I'm glad you're home. And you deserve to be in the boxroom for making me worry about you.'

'I think the punishment is a bit too harsh for the crime,' Tori grumbled as Poppy grabbed her bag and flew out of the kitchen. 'Love you!'

'Isn't it a bit early in our relationship to start throwing the L-word around?'

Tori whirled around to see Matt standing in the doorway, dressed in an old pair of jeans and a button-down black shirt, the cuffs rolled back from his wrists, his mobile in his hand. His damp hair was pushed off his face but he hadn't shaved, black stubble shadowing his jaw. He was magnificent naked and, in the weak early winter light pouring in from the kitchen windows, almost as sexy dressed.

Tori swallowed down a snarky retort and ignored his amused smirk. Resisting the urge to throw something at him, she pulled out a wide, fake smile and gestured towards the kettle. 'Morning. Would you like some coffee?'

A quick frown pulled his brows together. 'Sure.'

'Milk, sugar?'

'Black. Why are you being charming? Are you planning to throw something into it while I'm not looking?' Matt sat down in the chair she'd vacated and stretched out his long, long legs.

Don't tempt me, buster. But losing my temper again will only show you what a shrew I can be and you will never make another move on me if I act like a Macbeth witch. And I need you to invite me back into your bed so that I can shove the offer so far down your throat that your toes will bulge.

Tori smiled. 'I had a rough day yesterday and wasn't at my best.' *That was an understatement.* 'I misjudged the situation this morning so no harm, no foul.' Tori glossed over her epic temper tantrum and ignored his raised eyebrow. 'You are…obviously…unaccustomed to strange women rocking up in your bed and reacted badly.'

Matt's mouth quirked up. 'Not so unaccustomed,' he said under his breath. His mobile rang and he glanced down at it, twisting his lips. 'Excuse me while I take this.'

Tori listened with half an ear to his brief conversation, before turning away. *Oh, taking him down was going to be such fun.* She dumped coffee granules into his mug and threw some water into the cup. She placed the coffee mug on the table, deliberately leaning over his shoulder and allowing her arm to brush his. His body tightened in reaction and Tori saw—sensed—the shiver of attraction that ran through him. Not trusting her instincts, she walked to the chair opposite him, sat down and watched as his eyes, jade green this morning, drifted down her throat and flicked over her breasts as he wound up his call. She leaned back in her chair, draping an arm over the back, and knew that the action lifted her breasts against her tight purple long-sleeved T-shirt.

Yeah, take a good look at what you can't touch, dude.

Tori's mobile chirping from the table broke their eye contact and she picked it up and glanced at the text message. She frowned when she saw her mum's name on the display. Her mum never sent text messages and called even less frequently. Acknowledging that she had a daughter who was twenty-five-plus would mean admitting that she wasn't actually thirty-five herself, something Kay wasn't prepared to do.

Planning to meet up with your father at the end of the month in London. I suppose we should have lunch with you.

Suppose we should have lunch? Jeez, Mother, sound a little enthusiastic, won't you? I am your only child...

Matt lifted his cup and gestured with it. 'You okay?'

Tori sent him a cool look. 'Why wouldn't I be?' Apart from the fact that I have parents who suck?

'Your eyes...they went flat. Message from your creepy ex?'

'No,' Tori replied. 'But those should start up as soon as he is awake.' Tori saw his eyes drift down her chest and stop in the area she was pretty sure her nipples were lazing around.

'Hey! Want to bring your eyes up a foot or so?'

Matt's smile was slow. 'Toothpaste.'

'Sorry?'

'Toothpaste on your shirt. Oh, you thought I was checking out your rack. Sorry, no…do you normally dribble when you're brushing your teeth?'

Matt hid his smile in his coffee cup as Tori glanced down at her chest and her blush spread up her neck and into her face. She cursed, rather sexily, and jumped up and stormed out of the room. He watched her very, very fine ass walk away, knowing that her eyes were flashing with irritation.

Better irritation with him than the pain he'd seen in them earlier…

When she was out of sight he rubbed his hand across his face. He'd thought she was a knockout last night but in the light of day, even covered by clothes, she was enough to have his heart slamming into his ribcage in excitement. Stunningly exciting multicoloured hair—streaks of blondes, browns, reds—eyes the colour of a perfect African summer's night, a pert nose and a body that just wouldn't quit. A very impressive rack—he was going straight to hell for that lie, of course he had been looking at her breasts—a tiny waist, flared hips and legs that, as he'd seen last night, were long and lean.

She looked like a cover girl—that cheeky nose, full lips made for kissing and high cheekbones—but she was trouble, spelt in flashing capitals. Those guileless blue eyes were anything but innocent and he suspected that she'd pulled many an unsuspecting man into her craziness with her 'rescue me' or 'you're a big, strong man' look.

He wasn't fooled; there was something going on behind

those eyes and he suspected that whatever it was, or whatever she was planning, he would end up missing a chunk of his butt at the end of it.

No, Tori was up to something and he was too smart to fall for her tricks. After his not too delicate refusal of sex this morning he'd expected her to be anything but reasonable and charming and that made him suspicious.

Intrigued but very, very suspicious.

Tori re-entered the kitchen, her purple shirt replaced by an aqua shirt, its top buttons undone to show a hint of the lilac lacy bra she wore underneath. She'd slicked on a layer of gloss that highlighted that amazing mouth and he swore that there was a scent of jasmine now that hadn't been there earlier.

His crotch tightened in response.

Oh, yeah, she was playing him.

'So, are you here on holiday?' Tori asked, dropping two pieces of bread into an ancient red toaster. He wouldn't mind some toast but he was due to meet a potential new client at The Dorchester for breakfast in an hour or so. Later on this morning he wanted to check out a gym Alex had suggested; a place where guys went to do serious workouts and not ogle gym bunnies.

Not that there was anything wrong with ogling gym bunnies but it did cut into his workout routine...

'Sort of. A little work, a little play.' A lot more work and a lot less play. He had back-to-back meetings scheduled for most of the month; meetings to discuss product endorsements, a rehab centre he'd needed to check out for a football player who had a cocaine habit that was out of control, an anger management specialist he'd needed to brief for a pint-size gymnast who had an explosive temper. It was going to be a crazy month.

Tori's blue eyes darkened at his non-answer. 'So how do you know Isaac?'

Before he could answer Alex and Lara, the woman who'd knocked the ex-army officer off his feet, walked into the kitchen, their faces glowing from what had obviously been a very healthy bout of mid-morning sex.

Matt tried to squelch his jealousy. He had turned down the offer of morning sex… He eyed Tori speculatively, wondering if he'd been too hasty in turning her away. Her eyes slammed into his and he glimpsed something in her expression that had him frowning. Oh, yeah, she was still narked that he'd rebuffed her…

Tori liked to be in control of the situation and so did he. And it was high time she learnt that little girls didn't always get what they wanted.

'Oh, by the way, Lara and I are thinking of taking a holiday somewhere warm. We're sick of this dismal weather and we need some sun,' Alex informed them.

Matt sighed. He'd only been in London a couple of days and he was already missing the sun.

'When are you going?' Tori asked.

'Sadly, not for a few weeks yet. Maybe towards the end of the month,' Lara replied. 'Anyway, Alex and I thought that we might go out tonight. We could head to Red for a couple of cocktails and then go on to a club somewhere. I'm going to give Harry and Iz a call and see if they want to join us. And Poppy, obviously.'

'I think Poppy is on call so she won't go,' Alex said, sinking into a chair.

'Izzy is so happy and I adore Harry,' Matt heard Tori say to Lara and he picked up the wistfulness in her voice. 'You can just tell that they are going to make it, that they are going to be spectacular together.'

He shot her a look. Her eyes had turned softer and her bottom lip trembled. Now there was a hint of that softer, gentler personality he'd seen last night, the one beneath the sophisticated shell she was now parading, the one who didn't demand the limelight. For some deeply felt, probably crazy reason, he suspected that Tori seemed to need to be the centre of attention, the Queen Bee, centre stage and spotlighted. Matt sighed and ran his hand over his jaw. He did that all day every day for his clients. It was the last thing he wanted in a girlfriend or lover: too much hard work. It was even too much hard work for some easy sex...

A pity because, damn, she was hot.

'Alex, is there any chance of you going with me to Mark's to collect the rest of my stuff?' Tori asked.

Alex looked horrified. 'Why me?' he demanded, snatching a piece of toast from Tori's plate. 'He hates me.'

'Why does he hate you?' Lara asked, making them tea.

Tori took a while to answer, blushing as she did. 'Mark is—was—super-jealous and I made the mistake of telling him that Alex and I...we—once—a couple of times— did—had—' Tori looked embarrassed and avoided looking at Lara. Mmm, not quite as sophisticated as she liked to pretend to be.

Alex rolled his eyes. 'Hell, Toz, Lara knows that we had—' He sent Tori a puzzled look. 'What did you call it again?'

Tori's high cheekbones pinked up. 'Friends with benefits,' she mumbled.

Matt couldn't understand the flash of anger he felt, the twist of his gut, the contraction of his heart. He instinctively, categorically did not like the idea of Tori being under, over, in any way naked with Alex. He'd met the woman less than twelve hours ago, he shouldn't feel anything, especially not something that could be even distantly related to jealousy.

'Do you mind, Lara?'

Lara's eyes flashed with mischief and Matt decided that

he quite liked her. Hell, he quite liked all of them, even Tori. She had something he couldn't put his finger on that called to him even while she was making his groin twitch.

'Mind you borrowing Alex to haul luggage or for benefits?'

Tori looked startled, then her mouth split into the most genuine smile he'd seen from her yet at Lara's gentle teasing. It crinkled her eyes and suddenly the room was brighter and bolder. He now understood exactly what Alex meant about birds singing and mountains moving when she walked into a room.

His mum had been like that… Seriously, was he really comparing Tori to his mother? Where had his brains disappeared to?

'Just luggage hauling, I promise,' Tori replied to Lara's question before laughing, making his gut clench again.

'No problem. I have to get to work anyway; Saturdays are always busy,' Lara said, handing Alex his cup of tea. She winked at him before sitting in the chair next to Matt and placing her elbows on the table, her mug held in two hands. 'Are you going to join us tonight, Matt?'

Matt thought for a moment. 'I think so.'

'Good.' Lara sipped and spoke again. 'And how are you finding London?'

Matt met Tori's eyes and grinned as the memory of her gloriously naked body flashed behind his eyelids. He, very deliberately, looked her up and down and allowed his eyes to rest on her chest for about twenty seconds longer than was appropriate. 'Fine. The sights I've seen so far have been fabulous.'

Tori glowered at him and he knew that she knew that he was not referring to the Tower of London or Big Ben.

When she was certain that Lara's and Alex's gazes were not on her, Tori gently and, admittedly aristocratically, sent him a look designed to have his hands cupping his scrotum.

He smiled and she scowled. Despite his laid-back appearance and attitude, she would learn that he had a steel pair. And that it would take a lot more than a bold pair of eyes to bring him into line.

CHAPTER FOUR

MATT LEANED AGAINST the bar in Red, his big hand encircling his tumbler of whisky, and the glance he gave Tori was a long, slow lick of pure heat as she slid into the gap between him and an overdressed blonde who was desperately trying to grab his attention.

'That outfit for me, Stripes?' he drawled in his sunshine and sin voice. Her top was a tight black bustier that pushed her B-cup boobs into C-cup territory and her jeans were dark and tight and perfectly cut to make her legs look longer and skinnier and her butt rounder. Two-inch silver heels and a heavy silver cross nestled into her *hello-sailor* cleavage completed her outfit.

'You wish,' she retorted, thankful that the subdued light in the bar hid her flush. Look at him, she thought, in his faded jeans and a black vest over a white T. He looked both relaxed and sophisticated and so smooth that he could slide up walls. He made her skin prickle, Tori admitted. Prickle and heat and buzz…

Making love to him would be an incredible experience: those hard muscles under her touch, those green eyes heavy with passion, his long, thick erection…

No, no, no…she was not going to get all gooey and… and…and lusty over him. She had a plan and she was going to stick to it… Before she was finished with him, she'd have him begging for crumbs at her table and she'd walk away chuckling. Well, probably cackling...

The problem with Matt, apart from his drool-worthy body, Tori decided, was that he was a crazy combination of so laid-back he was practically horizontal but brutally observant with a healthy dose of very, very smart thrown in. Sexy and smart; it was a very, very dangerous mixture.

Matt lifted his glass up to his lips and Tori watched as the Adam's apple in his strong throat bobbed. 'Can I buy you a drink? Wine, champagne, a cosmopolitan?'

'Draught beer.'

Matt lifted an eyebrow. 'You are full of surprises, Stripes,' he said before placing the order.

'Why do you call me Stripes? Have you forgotten my name already?'

'I never forget the names of naked woman who end up in my bed and whom I don't sleep with.' He touched her hair, pulling a strand between his fingers. 'It's your hair... I love the streaks. I could call you Tiger if you prefer.'

'Tori works just fine too.' Tori tried to glare at him but she was still buzzing with pleasure from his complimenting her hair. And to be honest, how could she object to him calling her Stripes now? 'But if you call me Vicky I will castrate you.'

Matt's mouth twitched with amusement. 'Duly noted.'

Matt nodded his thanks as her beer was slid across the counter and Tori picked up the nod the bartender sent Matt and wasn't surprised when Matt kept his wallet firmly in his pocket. Mmm...was Isaac sponsoring Matt's stay in London? It was one of the priciest cities in the world and maybe he needed some financial help...maybe that was why he was staying in his flat, drinking on Isaac's dime. The outfit he wore tonight was nice but not flash and not a surprise since he wore either worn jeans or board shorts at home.

She was desperate to know more about him and she'd put her pride aside earlier to ask Alex about him but that had been like trying to draw blood out of a diamond. So she still didn't know whether Alex was being his normally reticent self or if Matt was taking some financial strain. She'd ask Poppy or Izzy but her normally gossipy friends were still talking about schizoid Mark and his aborted attempt for a threesome—she suspected it would be a while before she lived *that* down—and would immediately get on her case about her interest in Matt.

Thinking of Poppy and Izzy, she only realised now how much she'd missed her friends. She'd missed talking to them, laughing with them, sharing endless glasses of wine, Tori thought, glancing across the packed room and catching a quick glance of Izzy's golden head in the corner of Red. She seemed so happy and…complete with Harry. And Poppy seemed distracted…

Everything was changing, she thought, sucking her bottom lip between her teeth. It felt as if they'd all been tossed into another dimension where life-changing stuff happened. She'd moved out of the flat, Izzy had suddenly resigned from her job and fallen in love with Harry and Alex and Lara had hooked up.

Of course, the changes to their lives were positive and life affirming; hers not so much. Since she'd just dumped another boyfriend and had moved back into the boxroom it seemed as if they were moving forward and she backwards.

The story of her life.

Cue the violins for a pity party, she thought, forcing a smile onto her face. She might be feeling a little lost and a lot pathetic but nobody else had to know that but her.

Anyway, coming back to Matt… As Alex said, if she wanted to know anything about him then she should just ask the man.

'You're obviously not English. Where are you from?
Australia, New Zealand?'

Matt looked at her as if she'd sprouted two heads. Okay,
so she couldn't recognise individual accents from the col-
onies. Sue her.

'South Africa. Cape Town, to be precise.'

'Oh.' She wrinkled her nose, thinking about what she
knew of South Africa and Cape Town. Mandela, the end
of apartheid, Table Mountain…not much, obviously.

'And do you like it?'

'Cape Town? Yeah, I love it.'

She tried again. 'So what are you doing in London?
What do you do for a job, by the way?'

'I—'

A loud drum roll interrupted her thoughts and she
turned to look at the band in the corner. She grinned at
the lead singer, an Amy Winehouse lookalike with the
voice of an angel. In a moment her voice would slide over
the patrons and conversations would die down as every
eye, and ear, would turn to her. Tori still couldn't believe
that such talent was playing in a trendy Notting Hill bar
and not in Wembley Stadium.

Matt turned his back to the bar and Tori was well aware
of her bare shoulder pressing into his hard bicep, could feel
the heat of his body radiating into her side.

'She's damn good,' he said after the vocalist ended
her first song to an enthusiastic round of applause. 'She's
wasted here.'

'I was thinking exactly the same thing a little earlier
although I'm surprised that you can see it. Most people
would just think she's a good Amy impersonator.'

'I have a talent for spotting talent.'

'Most men think they do,' Tori said, her tongue very
firmly in her cheek.

'I actually can spot…' Tori placed her elbow on the

bar and looked up at him, her eyebrows lifted. Matt rolled his eyes and picked up his glass again and turned back to look at the band. Oh, she loved this song…she needed to dance. People were starting to crowd the dance floor and Matt nodded in that direction.

'Isn't that where you should be heading? Isn't that what you love to do?'

Tori lifted her hands in frustration. 'How? How do you know that I love to dance?'

Matt grinned. 'As soon as the music started your fingers started tapping against your thighs. Your hips did a tiny shimmy. I don't even think you knew you were doing it. You just reacted to the music…ergo, dancer.'

His words were spoken in that lazy river drawl but Tori shook her head in disbelief at his intuition and perceptiveness. It astonished her that he'd picked up, from tiny gestures, that she would normally be in the midst of the dancers, writhing and undulating, lost in the music and the movement.

'I…' She started to speak, not sure what to say. 'I… dammit.'

Tori didn't see Matt's grin as she stalked off, radiating frustration.

Moths to a flame. Bees to honey. Young, sharply dressed men watched her as she stalked her way onto the dance floor and within a minute she was surrounded by at least six guys who were jostling for her attention, hoping to catch her eye. Tori just smiled and started to flirt, batting her eyelashes and tossing her hair. Oh, she was good at it…

Matt's teeth ground together as he noticed the many masculine eyes watching her bump and grind on the dance floor. He knew her, he thought, or at least he knew the type. Hell, he'd dated many of her type. Exciting and unpredictable and probably high maintenance. He knew how to handle women, knew their quirks, their idiosyncrasies, their crazy, mostly unfounded insecurities.

He handled them professionally and he handled them in his personal life and he rarely let them affect him but no one had ever shoved a hand into his ribcage, grabbed his heart and squeezed it like Stripes.

And because of that, to keep his world turning on its axis correctly, he should be running as hard and as fast as he could in the opposite direction. He shouldn't be thinking about watching those magnificent eyes melt as he slid into her, shouldn't be imagining the tiny noises she made when she was turned on, her flushed-with-desire skin. Those long legs, perfect breasts, sexy mouth.

She was, physically, a knockout but something else drew him to her and he couldn't work out exactly what it was. Just when he thought he had her pegged—flighty, self-absorbed, flirtatious, attention-seeker—she did or said something or a look would flash across her face that had him questioning his instincts and wanting to dig deeper, to find out whether there were more layers below the party surface veneer.

Because he just knew that there were and they went deeper than most people suspected.

'Your eyes seem glued to my girl again, Cross.'

Matt looked to his right and lifted his head in Alex's direction and lifted his eyebrows at the comment. 'Your girl?'

Alex sipped his beer. 'Lara's the love of my life but that doesn't stop me being concerned about Poppy and Tori. Even Iz to an extent, although I like Harry.'

'Tori is…intriguing,' Matt reluctantly admitted.

'Yep, that's the problem. She's an A-grade flirt and acts as though she's as slick as an oil puddle but that's what she wants people to see. Interesting that you see something below that.'

'It's a pain in the ass,' Matt grumbled and Alex grinned.

'I should tell you that she grilled me about you all the way to Mark's house today. Why are you living rent free in the apartment? Do you have a job? Where were you from? Did any of us know anything about you other than that you are Isaacs's friend?'

Matt laughed. 'What did you tell her?'

'Not my place to tell her anything.' Alex looked uncomfortable. 'But because she's Tori, she probably jumped to a whole bunch of wrong conclusions when I didn't elaborate. She now thinks you are a bit down on your luck, that you're between jobs, having fallen on hard times.'

Ah, that was why she was trying to see how much money he had in his wallet and the questions about his job. 'Is she a wallet chaser?'

He'd be disappointed if she was. Not surprised but disappointed. Alex thought for a moment before shaking his head. 'No...Tori has many faults but being a gold-digger isn't one of them. She's actually a very successful PR consultant.'

Good to know. 'So, according to you, she's misunderstood and a pain?'

Alex shot Lara a look before turning back to Matt and smiling. 'Aren't they all? Until we get to know them and can't live without them?'

Yeah, well, he didn't know about that...he'd *never* know about that because he had no intention of being in that situation, of being at the mercy of his emotions over a woman.

Ever.

Tori wiggled her way into space between two guys at the bar, leaned forward and wrinkled her nose when she saw that the bartenders were at the other end and weren't in any hurry to make their way down to her end. And she was parched...

'I've been waiting for fifteen minutes already. I wouldn't hold my breath.'

Tori turned at the mournful voice to her right and looked into the thin face of a young guy standing next to her, his pale blue eyes miserable beneath the annoyance. Dressed in sharply creased blue jeans and a blue button-down, he screamed nerd and stood out like a sore thumb amongst the skinny jeans and tight T-shirt-wearing men of his own age. A good guy, Tori thought, instantly summing him up. Young, unsure, no confidence.

She knew how that felt…

She smiled at him. 'Not having fun?'

He twisted his lips. 'Not my scene. I'd rather be at home playing D and D.'

'So why are you here, then?' Tori asked him, interested despite herself. He looked a bit like a hot nerd… He had potential, she thought. Give him ten years and some muscle and he'd have no self-esteem issues.

'You irritating this girl, Bry?' The owner of the drawling voice clamped Bry on his shoulder and Tori could see his fingers digging into his flesh. Tori saw the barely concealed wince and her hackles rose as she met the insolent eyes of the other young man—skinny jeans and a tight T-shirt over a flabby stomach, yuck! 'My stepbrother hassling you, angel?'

Angel? Girl? She didn't think so. Tori narrowed her eyes at him, sent Bry a wink and lifted two fingers to her mouth. Everyone around her jumped as she let out a loud whistle that had Jake, her favourite bartender, lifting his head and ambling down to her side of the bar.

'Tori! What'cha want, hon?' Jake drawled.

Tori ordered two long necks, told Jake to put them on her tab, handed Bry one and grabbed his hand. 'You, gorgeous, are coming to dance with me.'

'Seriously?' Bry sputtered.

'Oh, yeah.' Tori dropped her voice and filled it with promise, tugging him into place behind her. She slid a look towards her friends and caught Matt's lifted eyebrows. Expecting to see censure and disapproval, and, at the very least, a whole bunch of jealousy, she frowned when she picked up none in his expression. She wondered if he had a jealous bone in his body. Maybe not if his amused expression was anything to go by. Why didn't this man do what he was supposed to? Did he enjoy being perverse?

Tori, the devil dancing inside, draped her arm around Bry's shoulders and smiled. She was going to boost a young guy's confidence, shove the jealous stick into his stepbrother's malicious eye and, hopefully by doing both, and if she was really lucky, irritate her green-eyed monster.

Except that when she looked back at him from the small dance floor, he was in animated conversation with a blonde beanpole wearing a scarlet strip of fabric around her hips that just covered her essential bits.

He wasn't remotely jealous or irritated. Or even looking at her.

But she was...doing all three. Grrr.

Back in the hallway of the flat at Lancaster Road, Tori watched Alex chase Lara down the passage as she slid out of her coat and stepped out of her heels. Her feet were screaming and she groaned as the muscles, cramped from being forced to pay the price, yet again, for beauty.

Poor feet.

Poor head too, Tori thought. She wasn't anywhere near being drunk but she had that slight buzz going that suggested that a headache was stealthily creeping closer. She'd take two aspirin and a well of water before she went to bed...

But that meant a couple of trips from the boxroom to the

bathroom every couple of hours and who could be bothered with that? She'd settle for the aspirin.

Tori shrugged out of her coat and hung it on a hook behind the door, draping it over a leather jacket that belonged to Alex, or Matt or even Isaac. Not so long ago there were only female coats on the hooks, now there were double the amount...

A large part of her wanted to go back to that time when Poppy had taken the leap to buy this flat and they'd eagerly agreed to rent from her so that she could make the payments on her eye-watering mortgage. They'd lived here so happily, the three of them in their feminine, eclectic, colourful flat. Men were allowed to visit but weren't encouraged to stay longer than the occasional sleepover.

'Tori?' Matt snapped his fingers in front of her face and Tori jumped when she came back to the present and the hard-eyed, hard-bodied man standing in front of her.

'Are you okay?' he asked, a frown of concern on his face.

Tori gave herself a mental slap and pulled up a smile. 'Sure, why wouldn't I be?'

'You were miles away,' Matt replied.

Tori shook her head, looked at the narrow door to the tiny boxroom and shuddered at the thought of that horrible bed. She looked at Matt, looking so relaxed and self-confident, and batted her eyelashes. It was worth a try. 'Can I sleep in your bed again? Your bed is so comfy and mine is so...not.'

Matt rolled his eyes. 'It can't be that bad,' he stated.

'No, it's worse.'

'Let's take a look.' He walked around the corner and opened the door to the boxroom. He had to turn sideways to enter the room and Tori followed him in, her nose to his back in the tiny space.

Matt shuffled himself around, his large frame in the

cramped space between the bed and the dresser, which was piled high with Tori's make-up and perfumes. A stainless-steel clothes rail stood at the bottom of her bed and was stuffed to capacity with her clothes.

Matt lifted his eyebrows. 'You have a *lot* of clothes.'

Tori didn't think that he'd appreciate the fact that this was only her basic wardrobe; she still had suitcases full of clothes in the attic where Alex had shoved them when they'd returned from Mark's flat.

Matt sat down on her bed the size of a gurney and lay back, his dark head on her pillow. His shoulders took up the width of the bed and his feet dangled off the end. He smiled up at Tori. 'You're right, it is bad.'

Tori pulled out the clip that secured her hair to her head and watched when Matt sucked in his breath when her curly hair tumbled down her back and flowed over the tops of her breasts. She had him right where she wanted him; if she couldn't get his motor running then she should just resign as a woman and join a convent or an ashram. Tori looked down at him and she could see his obvious reaction, see the long length of him telling her how happy he was to see her.

Wasn't his type? Yeah, right.

'Scoot up or else I'm going to have to lie on top of you,' she warned him, standing next to the bed, her hands on her hips.

Matt lifted his warm hand and his thumb brushed a small strip of flesh between the band of her jeans and the end of her bustier. She shivered in anticipation. The man had the ability to make goosebumps dance up and down her spine and make the saliva dry up in her mouth. Just from one simple, slow, crazy slide of the pad of his thumb over a thin strip of skin.

Who was seducing who here? Tori wondered.

'You have the most fantastic skin,' Matt whispered. 'Soft, silky, fragrant. So, so smooth.'

'Yours isn't too bad either,' Tori croaked, wishing he'd sit up and slide her zipper down and pay attention to other, far more interesting parts of her body. But, she reminded herself just in time, he wouldn't get that far because she was going to lead him down that happy path and at the last moment she was going to back away, leaving him with a massive hard-on...

No-o-o...

Hey, she reminded her protesting body, he rejected us! Remember?

We don't care about your pride, her body replied, we just want to get it on with Mr Hunky lying there.

Um, well, she had to agree.

Matt sat up, stood up and placed his big hands on either side of Tori's face. He tipped her head up and shook his head. 'You look exhausted...get some sleep, if you can in that torture device they call a bed. If I was you I'd bunk down on the couch.'

Tori looked at him with wide eyes, not understanding why he was still not taking her to bed. Dammit, did this guy need a gilt-framed invitation? A kick to his butt? What?

'Why are you doing this to me?' she whispered. 'Why don't you just take me upstairs and make love to me?'

Matt dropped a chaste kiss on her forehead. 'Sweetheart, I'll take you to bed when there are no ghosts between us. When you are so consumed with wanting me that there are no other thoughts in that overactive brain of yours besides what I'll do to you, how I'll make you feel.'

Tori closed her eyes as he stepped away and as soon as she said the words she wished she could yank them back. 'Aren't I enough for you?' she asked and hated the insecure note in her voice, the demand for reassurance.

Matt whirled around and within a heartbeat he had her pressed up against the chest of drawers, his mouth tangling with hers, the long, solid length of him touching her from chest to thighs. His hands were tunnelled in her hair and his mouth was plastered over hers, his tongue a warm, hot, wet slide in her mouth. She whimpered and twisted his shirt in her hands, then her hands flattened against his pecs, slid up the strong, tanned column of his throat, over his bristled jaw and back down again.

Matt did nothing but kiss her… His hands remained on her hips, pulling her up against him. Except from his thumbs finding that strip of bare flesh of her hip again, he didn't touch and she wanted him to. She wanted to get naked, now. Her hands started to undo the buttons on his shirt and she had two to go when one of his hands reached up and grabbed both of hers.

His mouth stilled on hers and Tori pulled back and forced herself to look up at him. 'What? Why have you stopped?'

Matt grabbed her jaw with his hand. 'Tori, look at me.'

Tori swallowed and looked up into those textured green depths. Beautiful eyes, beautiful man. Matt gave her jaw the tiniest of shakes as if he realised that her thoughts were veering off track. 'The question should be whether you think you are enough for *you*.'

Matt shut the door to the boxroom, whirled around the corner and sank down to the bottom step of the stairs leading to the turret room. He adjusted his crotch and blew out the breath he was holding. Holy hell, what was all that about? One moment he'd been on the bed, lazily touching her hip, and the next minute he had his tongue down her throat and was three seconds away from stripping her naked and taking her seven ways to Sunday.

Something about Tori shorted out his cerebral cortex

and rendered him suddenly incapable of making rational decisions. All he could think about was that made-for-sin body that he wanted to make his...

His? Where the hell did that come from? He'd never bought into the idea of love as possession, had never claimed ownership on any of his lovers, but the thought of Tori being with someone else, physically, made him want to punch a fist through the wall. He was losing his mind, he decided. It was the only reasonable explanation for feeling this way about a girl he barely knew.

She was the type he normally avoided like the plague... far too concerned about what people thought about her and how she was perceived. Innately stylish and impeccably dressed, which suggested that she was vain and more than a little self-absorbed. Possibly a bit of a doormat when it came to men, if all the titbits that he'd picked up from his housemates were true...

The type of girl who became whoever her current boy-friend wanted her to be.

But there was something about her that intrigued him and he didn't like it...and he certainly didn't like the fact that his pants got all perky whenever she was around. And the bitch of it was that it wasn't all physical; physical he could ignore—he'd refused passes from countless woman over the years—but something, somewhere inside that pretty package, called to him.

Dammit, he just wished he knew what it was so that he could get it to stop!

Matt rested his wrists on his bent knees and stared at his flat boots. He'd learned, at a very early age, that loving a woman could have huge, painful consequences. Death being the most excruciating and gut-wrenching conse-quence of all. So he'd never been in love, never allowed himself to fall down that rabbit hole. He had firsthand ex-perience with the devastation it could convey.

Enough…enough now.

He should go upstairs, shower off the club smell and get some sleep. He had a meeting with the rehab clinic in the morning and marketing execs of an energy drink company to deal with in the afternoon…

Matt was about to stand up when he heard the door to the boxroom open and he held his breath as Tori rushed out of her hutch and slammed on brakes when she saw him sitting on the stairs.

She slapped her hands on her hips and sent him a belligerent look. 'Whoop-dee-do, you are still here. How much luckier can I get?'

Matt was quite sure that he could sell that tone as a fantastic way to strip wallpaper. Sending her a wary look, he watched as she started to walk down the passage to the bathroom. Tori stomped away, cursed, turned on her heel and stomped back again. Matt hoped that the others were already asleep because her feet made enough sound to wake the dead.

'What did you mean by that crack?'

Matt cocked his head and pretended innocence. 'What crack?'

'That statement you made about me being enough for me! What does that even mean?'

The tone could strip wallpaper but her laser glare could jackhammer concrete. He far preferred this riled-up version of Tori to the fake, fashion-girl persona she seemed to pull on like a cloak. He lifted one shoulder in a take-it-or-leave-it shrug before leaning back on one elbow and sending her a penetrating look. 'Why did you kiss me, Victoria?'

Tori's gaze, if it was at all possible, narrowed even further. 'Because that is something people do who are attracted to each other.'

Matt kept his voice gentle, knowing that if he raised his

voice he'd lose her and control of this conversation. 'Are you attracted to me or are you using me to forget your ex or as some sort of payback because he dumped you? Is sleeping with me a way to lift your middle finger at him? Or proving to yourself that you are worthy because a man finds you attractive?'

Her mouth opened in an instinctive denial and then she pulled the lie back and lifted one shoulder. 'I don't know. Maybe...probably. I'm just so damn angry and confused.'

'And you thought that hopping into bed with me was a viable idea? Hell, Tori.' Matt stood up and leaned his shoulder into the wall. 'What your ex did to you was cruel but *he* did it, believe it or not, and his actions have nothing to do with you. But how you react to what he did is on you.'

Tori rubbed her forehead in confusion. 'You're talking in riddles, Matt.'

It was far too late for a life-coaching session but Matt thought he'd give it one more try. 'Life is about choices and you can either choose to learn from what he did or feel sorry for yourself and ignore your pain by burying it in meaningless sex with me.'

'I vote for the meaningless sex,' Tori muttered.

'When sleeping with me is not about anger and payback and as a way for you to stop feeling crappy, I'm upstairs behind the door on the right,' Matt told her, before dropping a kiss on her cheek and walking up the stairs. 'Come and find me then.'

CHAPTER FIVE

TORI WHIRLED INTO Ignite on the next morning and waved at Marco, the maître d', as she headed towards their favourite table by the huge alfresco windows. This was just like old times, she thought, Sunday breakfast with Poppy and Izzy and…Lara.

Lara too? How did she feel about that? For so long it had just been the three of them and now Lara was a constant presence in the flat and, because they all loved Alex, she would be in their lives for a long time to come.

But she liked Lara; she didn't really know her but she made Alex happy, so how could she not?

Tori bent down to kiss Izzy's cheek and give her a squishy hug and, because she was still feeling a bit raw after her collision with the Green-Eyed Monster, kissed and hugged Poppy and, to Lara's surprise, repeated the gesture with her.

God, how could she survive without her girlfriends?

'Tori's back…' Izzy sing-songed, and reached for the bottle of champagne and poured the fizzy wonderfulness into a glass. They didn't bother with the orange juice; there was simply no need to mess with perfection.

'Dear God, I need this,' Tori said after taking a healthy sip.

'It's been far too long since we all had breakfast together,' Poppy agreed, lifting her glass. 'Here's to Tori dumping the sex-addict sociopath.'

'Here's to that!' Tori agreed.

Izzy's eyes danced with mischief as she leaned forward and lowered her voice. 'Truth or dare?'

Tori rolled her eyes. How old were they? Twelve? 'Truth.'

'It's something I've been dying to know... Did Mark really try on your underwear?'

She scowled. 'Trust *you* to remember that.'

Lara shuddered. 'He did *what*?'

Tori closed her eyes and flushed a bright red. Then she looked at Lara. 'Do you remember that massive order I placed with you?'

'Sure. I was ecstatic at the sale but a bit miffed because you weren't exactly excited by the idea,' Lara replied.

'I bought all that stuff because I borrowed Mark's computer to do something, saw a file on his desktop entitled "Tori lingerie" and thought they were pics of me. Uh no... they were pics of Mark, all dressed up in my lingerie and... raring to go.'

Poppy slapped a hand across her mouth. 'He had an erection?'

'Yeah...not one of my fondest memories,' Tori stated quietly. Dear God, why hadn't she left him then? Wasn't that a big freaking clue that the wheel was turning but his hamster was dead?

'Eeeewwww!' Izzy winced. 'Dear Lord, most of your boyfriends have sucked but Mark is reaching new heights of ick.'

'Sorry, Tori,' Lara added quietly, sending Tori a supportive smile.

'So I tossed all my lingerie and bought new from Lara. And I told him that I'd kill him if he touched it.'

'Maybe next time you should pick a man who isn't small

enough to fit into your lingerie,' Izzy suggested. 'And a man who doesn't cheat, isn't into the kinky stuff…maybe someone *normal*?'

'Good point, I'll keep that in mind.' Tori looked up as Marco approached them and, after much discussion and flirting, he left with their breakfast orders.

'I hit on Matt,' Tori said into the lull of conversation. She stared out of the window, watching the light rain fall on the heads of people passing by. When her friends said nothing, she shrugged and looked across the table to Izzy and Poppy. 'He's turned me down twice.'

Izzy frowned. 'He doesn't want to sleep with you? Pffff. Clearly not into women, then.'

Tori, remembering his eyes heating with appreciation of, well, her, lifted her glass, took a sip and put it down again. 'No, he's not gay. The first time he refused was after I cried and the second time he said that I was using him as some sort of way to punish Mark.'

Tori looked out of the window again and missed the long look that Izzy and Poppy exchanged. 'You cried?' Poppy said. 'You never cry.'

Tori shrugged. She could spin the story of climbing into Matt's bed naked and have them laughing like drains in five minutes but she didn't want to, not this time. 'He caught me at a bad time.'

'Were you using him?' Izzy demanded.

Tori chewed the inside of her lip. 'I don't know…I don't seem to know anything anymore! He's incredibly attractive…so cool, calm and collected but so perceptive. He has a steel-trap mind under that layer of laid-back, but he sees too much. Besides, he's not my type.'

'He's hot and he's breathing,' Izzy stated. 'That's your type.'

'He's muscled and super-sporty—you know I only like poets and dreamers!'

'Since when?' Poppy demanded. 'And Mark was a pervert not a poet.'

'Mark owns a gallery and I'm drawn to the creative souls,' Tori argued, knowing she was on shaky ground with this argument. 'Anyway, Matt doesn't seem to do anything. He's in the flat at odd times of the day and he lounges around the house in board shorts and T-shirts—'

'It is centrally heated,' Lara pointed out.

'He must be a frustrated surfer or ski-instructor, something stupid,' Tori decided.

Tori missed Izzy's sarcastic smile. 'Yeah, that's it.'

'He doesn't seem to have much money,' Tori said, warming to her theme. 'He hardly drank last night and he's crashing in Isaac's room for free. I think he's a freeloader and annoying—'

'Yeah, that's *not* it,' Izzy quietly stated.

'Your annoyance with him couldn't possibly have anything to do with your pride and him turning you down twice, could it?' Poppy jumped into the conversation.

Tori narrowed her eyes at Poppy before picking up one of Marco's small bread rolls and lobbing it at Poppy's head.

'Mees Veeectoria!' Marco shouted from across the room. 'You cannot throw zee food!'

'I hate you,' she grumbled, blushing when the other breakfast patrons turned to look at her. Leaning back in her chair, she sipped her champagne and looked at Izzy. 'I'm so jealous of you, Iz, and of you, Lara.'

'Good grief, why?' Izzy asked.

'You are both so happy, so in love. I want that... I crave a love that's ocean deep. You two seem to have it,' Tori said quietly. 'I want someone who says I love you every night and proves it every day. Instead I have a relationship with a bucket of ice cream.'

'Me too,' Poppy stated, waving her glass around. 'I want what she said.'

'Poppy, you actually have to engage with a man to have a man, darling. You know…date, put yourself out there.' Izzy wielded the champagne bottle again and pinned Tori to her seat with an intense look. 'The problem with you, Toz, is not that you don't have enough love but you are always giving it to the wrong damn person. Because of your crappy parents, you associate love with drama. I'm just so scared that one of these days a nice, good man is going to tell you he loves you and, because it doesn't come with craziness and angst, you're going to run in the opposite direction.'

'No, I won't,' Tori hotly replied. 'Being loved like that is what I want.'

Izzy shook her head as if she didn't believe her. Tori saw that she was about to argue and caught the cautionary hand that Poppy laid on Izzy's arm. When had they started to pussyfoot around her? When had she pulled so far away that her friends couldn't be honest with her?

'Talk to me, please. Say what you want to say,' Tori pleaded, suddenly scared that she'd damaged these relationships too. They were the most important in her life and if she had, she'd never forgive herself. 'We've always been honest—please don't stop now.'

Izzy lifted her eyebrows at Poppy, who nodded briefly. 'Stop chasing love and attention and demanding it from men who can't give it to you. If it's not freely given then it isn't worth having.'

She knew that…didn't she? Or maybe it was just another of those things that she grasped on an intellectual basis and not emotionally. There seemed to be quite a few of those popping up lately.

'Can I say something too?' Lara asked. 'I know it's not really my place but—'

'One more punch to the face won't hurt,' Tori quipped, looking at Izzy, who pulled a tongue at her.

'I know I don't know you well but I've listened to these two and Alex talking about you and I was thinking that you seem to think that a relationship is for getting stuff—'

'Isn't it? Love? Security? Sex? Happiness?' Tori wrinkled her nose in confusion.

Lara shook her head. 'A relationship—love—is about giving, not getting, Tori. It's also about them, making them feel happy and secure, and it's not always about you.'

The table fell silent and the three childhood friends stared at Lara, with varying degrees of surprise on their faces. Poppy recovered first and she lifted her champagne glass in Lara's direction. 'Oh, I like you. My brother, as the Yanks would say, did good.'

Every year the PR firm of Blatt, Blatt and King, one of the premier PR companies in London, joined up with their sister company, BB&K's events company, and a charity of choice to host a celebrity charity event. They had outdone themselves this year, Tori thought in satisfaction, looking at the catwalk celebrities. Her work on the event was done; she'd PR'ed the hell out of it. Every celebrity and socialite in London was in the room, society and entertainment reporters were eavesdropping and prominent sporting and business people were mingling.

Standing at the back of the room, partially obscured by a large palm, she actually had a better view of the catwalk than most of the guests. Tori, dressed in her favourite black cocktail dress—sexy but understated, she was working—caught the eye of the managing director of BB&K and smiled when he lifted his champagne glass in her direction. It was all the acknowledgement she'd get for a job well done but she knew that he had a razor-sharp brain and that her good work wouldn't be forgotten when it came to employee appraisals at the end of the year.

'I just thought you should know that you have the most amazing legs.'

Tori turned to her left and caught the eye of a tall blond holding two flutes of champagne. 'Champagne?' he asked, lifting a glass.

Smooth pick-up line, Tori thought. She'd heard a lot worse over the years from men who were a lot further down the evolutionary ladder than this specimen. Tall, broad shoulders, he was the perfect clothes horse for that expensive suit. Amused, brown eyes, clean-shaven and a deep voice.

Hottie factor of six thousand and fifty-two. 'I'm Ben Holden,' he told her, handing her the champagne flute, and she picked up a note of expectancy in his voice. Should she know who he was?

Did it matter? He was cute, had a great smile and, if his opening line was anything to go by, a great deal of charm.

The MC saved her from answering by opening the ceremony and, because he was both funny and mercifully brief, the first celebrity strutted down the ramp. The soap-opera star flashed her mega-watt smile and slinky body and the room erupted in applause. Tori glanced down at her programme: actors and actresses, athletes, rugby players, rock stars, tennis stars… They'd each given up their time to help raise money for scholarships for inner-city children.

Nice of them.

'And you are?'

'Tori.' She shook his hand.

Ben tipped his head to one side as she quickly withdrew her hand and looked back towards the stage. 'Hello, terrific legs Tori.'

Tori laughed lightly. 'Thanks.'

'Oh, it's so my pleasure.' His lips quirked up into a killer smile and her belly fluttered. There it was, that buzz of attraction. Found you.

'Listen, I have people to meet, greet. What do you think about hooking up later? We could go back to my hotel, start with a drink and I could try to impress you with my witty repartee. We'll see where it goes from there.'

'Yeah…I…' Lord, she was tempted. A couple of hours of flattery, attention, maybe some hot kisses and strong arms. He'd flirt with and charm her, make her laugh and she'd bask in his attention, in his interest. She'd feel pretty and interesting and appreciated. How long had it been since a handsome man had made her feel like a million dollars?

And why do you need *a man to make you feel like that, Victoria?*

She wasn't sure whose voice popped into her head— Poppy's? Izzy's?—but the words pulled her up short, stopped her in her tracks. Tori bit her lip in horror. Was she actually considering walking out of a work function to spend a couple of hours with a stranger so that she could feel better about herself? Just for some masculine attention?

Any attention?

Was she insane? What the hell was wrong with her?

Tori felt the bite of tension skitter through her. She wasn't interested in him because he was good-looking and charming; she was interested in him because she thought that he could make her feel better.

That was…*sad*. Desperate. Needy. God, she was suddenly an object of her own pity.

Sometimes she really didn't like what she saw, didn't like who she was…and this was *it*. She was *done*. She was not going to behave like that any more, be that insecure, desperate-for-attention woman any more. She'd allowed men to cheat on her, disrespect her, wear her damned lingerie and this—casual invitations from strange men—was how it all started. She felt utterly humiliated at her lack of self-respect.

'Wow, I have no idea what just happened in that head of yours but I can see that the answer is no,' Ben drawled.

Tori pulled a face, embarrassed. 'Sorry,' she murmured and sighed in relief when he walked off.

Tori placed a hand on her sternum and breathed, watching him walk away. It felt good, she felt good... At twenty-six, nearly twenty-seven, she was finally looking at herself clearly. Maybe, just maybe she was done with acting like a teenager when it came to men. She was not going to confuse attention with affection any more and she was not going to look for love in all the wrong places again.

It was high time she started to act with the dignity of a woman and not the wild impulsiveness of a girl. And that meant finding out who she was without a man, what defined her, what made her happy...who exactly Victoria Phillips was.

And it also meant no more men, not for a while...

Tori felt a prickle between her shoulder blades and lifted her head. A broad shoulder pressed into hers as a glass of champagne was pushed into her hand. She looked up, her jaw falling open as a pair of amused green eyes laughed at her.

'What are you doing here?' she snapped. Matt, her ratty-board-short wearing, annoying flatmate was the last person she expected to be at this event; she and her friends did not socialise in such elevated society. And he was wearing...her eyes flicked over his expensive tux...Armani? Hugo Boss? No, definitely Armani...

Guess her assumptions about him having no cash, of being a freeloading surfer, were way, way, *way* off the mark. To be here he had to fork out some serious money for a ticket, which were harder to obtain than fist-size diamonds.

'I have a couple of clients who are celebrity models...' Matt replied, gesturing to the stage where a very eques-

trian-looking woman was modelling a slinky gold ball
gown. 'Maya Bennet being one.'

'She's your client?' Tori hissed, her mind operating at
warp speed. Client? What could Matt do for Maya Bennet? Hairdresser, stylist, accountant? Gigolo? Her eyes
narrowed to slits. 'What exactly do you do, Cross?'

'I'm her agent.'

'Meaning?'

'I source and negotiate the most lucrative contracts for
her and my other clients.' He grinned as a tall, muscular
man accompanied a tiny, and famous, ballroom dancer
onto the catwalk. 'That's Drew Manning, legendary rugby
player. He's another of my clients. And a good friend.'

Huh, she thought, trying to wrap her head around this
tuxedo-wearing, sharp, successful version of Matt.

'So that explains what I am doing here... Your turn,'
Matt said.

She wanted to ask him why he was staying at the flat,
what else he was doing in London, ask him about his other
clients. But he was waiting for an answer so she shrugged.
'The firm I work for co-ordinates this event. I did the PR.'

Matt looked around and nodded. 'Seems like you did
a damn good job.'

Tori flushed under his praise. 'Thank you. And, on
that point, I should tell you that I am working tonight...'

She allowed her sentence to drift off and hoped that
Matt would pick up her hint. His eyes crinkled in amusement. 'So, no dirty dancing, sexual innuendo, biting re-
marks? Is that why you blew off Ben Holden?' Matt asked.

'That too. Is he someone I should have recognised?'

Matt shrugged. 'Maybe, if you are into sports, which
you are obviously not. Cricket player, model, does a bit
for kids' charities.'

'Is he a client? Ben?'

'Nope. So, why did you blow him off?'

Tori lifted her eyebrows. 'Who says that I did?'

'Because if you said yes, he'd still be here protecting his turf and stopping another guy from trying the same thing.' Matt shrugged at her perplexed look. 'It's a guy thing.'

'If you say so. And yes, I did blow him off.'

'Why?' Matt persisted. 'He's good-looking, he's successful, he's actually a nice guy.'

Because he knew most of the details of her break-up with Mark, because she'd cried on his shoulder, she felt as if she could tell him a little of what she was thinking earlier. 'I'm taking a break from men, trying to sort my head with regard to the penis-toting half of the species.'

'Ah. That working for you?'

'I'll let you know.' Tori dredged up a wide smile and waved her still-full glass and nodded in Drew Manning's direction. 'Dang that he's married. I've had the biggest crush on him for ever.'

'You and every other woman in the world,' Matt said. Tori raised her eyebrows at his brusque tone and his quick frown. If she knew men, and she did, then Matt sounded a little jealous...of Drew? Or, her heart rate bumped up, of her crush on Drew? Mmm, interesting...

Except that she couldn't do anything about exploring that little nugget of interesting because she was, as of fifteen minutes ago, taking a break from flirting with men to get her head screwed on straight...and men included Matt Cross.

She might be on a time-out but she hadn't managed to get rid of that devil on her shoulder who frequently led her into trouble. 'Can I meet him?'

Matt's frown deepened. 'He's married, Stripes.'

'Geez, I'm not going to proposition him, Matt.' She stuck her tongue in her cheek. 'Well, not much, anyway.'

'Behave yourself, Victoria,' Matt threatened, his green eyes as hard as soapstone.

Tori sighed and looked up at the ceiling. This was the problem with having a reputation as—at best—a very skilled flirt. People battled to tell when she was joking. Still…it hurt that Matt would instinctively think the worst of her. She sighed heavily. 'Believe it or not, but I have always left married men alone. I was *kidding*, Matt.'

'Oh.' Matt sipped his champagne and wrinkled his nose. 'God, I hate this stuff.'

Tori looked at her glass longingly. 'I love it but I can't drink it… It goes straight to my head.'

'And you're working.' Matt turned to put his glass on the high table behind them. When he resumed his place next to her, he folded his arms. 'So, am I included in your man embargo?'

'You're a man, aren't you?' she pertly replied.

Tori shot him a quick glance and wrinkled her nose. He was the one she had to be the most careful of. She didn't like the tremors he put in her stomach, the prickle of heat he caused on her skin. Her shortened breath, the throb of lust she felt deep in her womb. Her body was blithely ignoring the memo her brain and heart sent about men: that she should keep her distance. Her body wanted to get up close and very personal with Matt and this time it had nothing to do with payback or forgetting Mark, nothing to do with looking for temporary love or affection.

This was simple, flat-out attraction and it scared her panties off her. Honestly, she could feel her G-string melting from one look from those hot green eyes. That hot stare that had her licking her lips, wishing she could reach over and dismantle that silky black tie, undo the buttons on his shirt.

'Yeah, you're getting there…' Matt muttered.

Huh? 'Getting where?' she asked, her eyes on his mouth. 'Matt!'

Matt jerked his eyes off Tori's face and his mouth

curved in a smile as he stuck his hand out to the man who'd approached them while they were eye locked. Drew Manning...tall, built, hunky and yet not half as sexy as Matt. Huh. How had that happened? A month ago she thought Drew was sex on a stick but now...not so much. Not when she compared him to Matt with his wicked eyes and crooked smile.

'Meet Tori Phillips. She organised this event.' Matt gestured to her and his look clearly told her to behave herself and not to act like a chump. It was tempting to wind him up and then she remembered that she was working and wasn't she trying to be more grown up?

So instead of batting her eyelashes, she stuck out her hand, gave Drew a small smile and spoke in a normal, non-flirty voice. 'Hi, nice to meet you. Thanks for doing the catwalk thing.'

Drew pulled a face. 'Yeah, so not my thing but it was for charity. Congratulations on organising the event—you do good work.'

Tori thanked him graciously and carried on a normal conversation with one of the legends of international rugby and Matt tried to keep his jaw from hitting the floor. Gone was the vamp, the flirt, and a normal, professional... charmingly erudite woman stood in front of him, having a normal conversation with one of his most famous clients.

He'd seen women dissolve into puddles of nonsense when confronted with Drew, and Tori, who not ten minutes before had confessed to having the hots for the man, was doing the exact opposite. She was behaving with dignity and...and...class. She had class oozing out of her fingertips.

So, that was a big surprise. As was her obvious professionalism, her excellent work—he'd heard many comments of how well organised and publicised this event was—and her intelligence. He'd missed that...and that was even more of a shocker.

He never missed anything…

He'd suspected that there were layers to Tori but he hadn't expected them to go this deep. And that made the earth move beneath his feet… Sexy and hot he could deal with, smart and competent were a bit more than he was willing to handle.

Matt was still deep in thought when he felt a feminine hand on his arm and he turned to look down into the gorgeous face of one of his other favourite clients, Maya Bennet. He bent to kiss her cheek and smiled when she kept her cheek up against his to murmur in his ear, 'Hello, handsome.'

'Hello, gorgeous,' he replied, grinning at her when she stepped back. Despite being the reformed bad girl of horse riding, she still had a bit of a wild streak that he liked.

Maya turned to look at Drew, her mouth curving in a fond smile. 'Hello, Drew. Where's your lovely wife?'

Drew dropped a kiss on her temple and tipped his head to the blonde heading their way. 'On her way. Matt told me that you are engaged…congratulations.'

'Thank you.' Maya held out her hand to Tori and Matt introduced them quickly. Maya bit the inside of her lip and looked from Drew to Tori. 'The engagement is not general knowledge but it will be soon… We just need to manage the damned press. It's going to be a circus.'

Matt gripped Maya's shoulder in reassurance. 'That's my job to worry about, Maya, not yours. You just be happy and I'll sort out the press.'

Maya nodded but Matt could see the worry in her eyes. When the press heard that the world's most famous, gorgeous equestrian was marrying the world's most famous racing driver, they would go insane. And it was his job to manage the process of informing the world… Just the thought gave him a headache. That was another reason why he was in London: he needed someone to help him manage the process.

Tori caught his eyes, twirled her finger around and mouthed 'PR' at him. Matt narrowed his eyes…and she shrugged.

'I can help you manage the process,' she said, grabbing her champagne glass off the table and taking a healthy sip. 'Think about it.' Tori lifted her glass and sent them a smile. 'It was so nice meeting all of you. Thank you for contributing to the success of this evening.'

Matt watched her walk away, her swaying hips causing her sexy dress to swish, her legs long and sexy in thin black stockings and sky-high heels. He could imagine her standing in front of him naked except for those stockings, garter belt and shoes and the saliva in his mouth disappeared.

Drew pushed a fresh glass of champagne into his hand and slapped his back.

'Close your trap, Cross, you look like a dork.'

CHAPTER SIX

TWO DAYS AFTER the charity auction, Tori was in her office, swamped with paperwork and desperately trying to finish her report on the function. It wasn't going well because whenever she thought of that night the image of a sexy sports agent in a tuxedo flashed behind her eyes and sent her off into an X-rated daydream that she absolutely should not be having at work.

As a result the report was taking six times longer than it should and if she didn't get cracking then she'd be late for dance class. The report was due in today and—she looked at her watch—it was fifteen minutes before closing time.

Tori sighed when her mobile vibrated on her desk and she considered not answering it. But she was genetically unable to ignore a ringing phone so she pressed the green button to activate the speaker phone. 'Tori speaking.'

'Stripes? It's Matt.'

Whoa…! Daydream about the devil and he calls. Wow… why was he calling? She hadn't seen him since the night of the charity auction when he'd left in a group of exceptionally good-looking athletes and celebs without so much as a look at her over one broad shoulder. She hadn't seen him at home either and when she'd casually asked Poppy where he was, she'd heard that he was away for a couple of days.

'Tori?' Matt's voice bumped her out of her thoughts.

'Sorry, Matt, hi. What's up?'

'I'm downstairs at your reception area and your fierce keeper of the gates wouldn't let you know that I'm in the building because I don't have an appointment. Can I come up?'

Tori sent a worried look at her monitor where the dreaded report mocked her. 'I have so much work to get through, Matt.'

'It's important, Tori, and I'll make it worth your while.' Matt's deep voice vibrated through her ear and down to her womb. Through the floor-to-ceiling glass of her office windows and door she could see the rest of the BB&K staff shutting down their computers and pulling on their coats. It was five-thirty on a Friday evening and no one would be staying late.

She'd be alone with Matt and that so wasn't a good idea, especially since she was having triple-X-rated fantasies about what she wanted to do with that body.

'Come on, Stripes.'

Tori sighed, knowing that there was no way she could say no. 'I'll call down to Sally and ask her to let you up. Third office on the right on the fourth floor.'

Tori used the five minutes she knew she had to quickly brush out her hair, spritz on some perfume and she was just slicking on some lipstick when she heard the lift open and the normal chatter of her colleagues drop off. Oh, yeah, sexy Matt Cross had a way of silencing females. She knew without looking that they'd be standing there—possibly mouths agape—their eyes radiating curiosity.

Tori walked to her door and sent the staff a hard look. She waved them towards the lifts. 'Goodnight, have a good weekend.'

Since she was technically their boss, the women sent Matt one last curious look and reluctantly stepped into the lift. Only after the doors closed and she saw the lights moving did she sigh and turn to Matt with a tired smile. 'Hi. Sorry about them—you'd think that they'd never seen a good-looking man on this floor before.'

Matt stepped forward and kissed her cheek before shrugging out of his thigh-length woollen black coat. Under the coat he wore a dark grey suit, a deep blue shirt and a blue and white striped tie. He looked smart and professional and...tired, she realised. Utterly drained.

Tori led him into her office and gestured for him to sit down on her red and white striped couch. 'Would you like some coffee?'

Matt draped his coat over the back of the couch, undid the button holding his suit jacket together and slowly sat down. 'I don't suppose you have any whisky in your bottom drawer, do you?'

'Sorry.'

'Coffee, then.' Matt pulled his tie down, undid the collar button and rested his head against the back of the couch.

'You look exhausted,' Tori said, heading towards her coffee machine and fixing him a black espresso. She knew he needed the punch of caffeine.

'I am. I've been in Glasgow, trying to persuade a client to go into rehab. He has a wicked cocaine habit that is threatening his career.'

Tori passed him the cup, which he gratefully took. 'Were you successful?'

'Well, he said that he would go. Whether he stays there and it takes is up to him. If he remains sober, I remain his agent. If not we're history,' Matt said, closing his eyes. 'Unfortunately, I don't think it will take. People only change when they know that they have to or when they have been hurt enough that they need to.'

Like me, Tori thought. She had been hurt enough, mostly at her own hand, that she wanted to make some changes. Of course, it was nothing like having a raging coke habit but she was starting to feel proud of the strides she had made.

She was trying not to be impetuous anymore and was taking some time to get her bearings; she wanted to do this right but her biggest problem was sitting right in front of her: hot, sexy and very, very alluring. She felt drawn to Matt as she'd never felt drawn to a man before and she didn't want to be. She wanted to be smart and thinking about her choices about men.

It was just so damn difficult because he wasn't only the best-looking man she'd come across…ever…but he was also smart and successful. Everything she'd spent the past five years wishing her men were, hoping they would turn out to be.

Dammit to hell and back.

Tori sat in the bucket chair and crossed her legs. 'Why are you here, Matt?'

Matt placed his cup on the coffee table between them and rested his arms on his thighs. 'I need some help, actually. Professional help.'

'Maya Bennet and her mystery fiancé,' she calmly stated even though her heart was pounding. She quivered in expectation. Managing the PR around Maya and her fiancé would be a massive coup for her professionally.

'I've been spending a lot of time discussing how to manage this with Maya. We've decided that we have to hold a press conference, to give the bottom feeders an opportunity for photos, to allow access to them for a reasonable amount of time…maybe a day.'

Matt sighed at his ringing mobile, picked it up and quickly spoke. 'I'll call you back in a half-hour. Yeah, I'll explain the endorsement deal then.'

Matt's clients never stopped with the phone calls, she thought, even though her head was spinning from his proposal. 'A weekend would be better. I'd carefully and deliberately choose the photographers and the journalists and I'd hold it at a small country hotel where their access could be controlled. A press conference in the morning, one-on-one interviews in the afternoon, some separately, some together. A photo shoot the next morning.' Tori reached backwards, grabbed a notepad and a pen from her desk and jotted a couple of names on the top page, writing the corresponding magazines and tabloids the journalist represented. 'Those are my top-line thoughts. I might have more.'

Matt took the pad and looked over the names. 'Teri Matthews is a paparazzo.'

'But he's independent and respected and not quite as much of a slime ball as everyone else.'

Matt rubbed the back of his neck. 'This is why I needed help.'

Tori leaned back in her chair. 'But surely you have a PR person who deals with your day-to-day needs? Your clients are high profile—this can't be the first time you've needed PR.'

Matt stood up and headed back to her coffee machine, jamming the cup under the spout and pushing the button. 'Yeah, my relationship with the company I was using went south.'

Although she was curious, Tori knew better to ask which company he had been using. And why.

'The last consultant I worked with got very demanding and eventually gave me an ultimatum to do her or to take my business elsewhere. I took my business elsewhere.'

Oh, jeez. Tori felt her face flame and scrunched up her face when he lifted her chin up to look into her eyes. 'I don't have a problem mixing business with pleasure, Stripes—as adults we should be able to separate one from the other. But I'll be damned if I'll be manipulated.'

'Okay. She was stupid if she didn't think you would call her bluff.'

'Very.' Matt's hand still held her chin.

'Relax, Matt, I have no intention of hassling you to sleep with me again,' Tori said, bravely.

'Damn, because I think the timing is much better now. Oh, well…now I'll just have to chase you instead of the other way around.' Matt dropped his hand, flashed her a smile, turned away and went to study a small abstract oil painting on her wall.

'Matt, seriously…I'm trying to avoid stupid situations with men and give myself a break from constantly making a fool of myself. I know that I propositioned you twice but I really am taking a break.'

'You're taking a break from looking for love, for a relationship.' Matt turned and jammed his hands into the pockets of his suit trousers. He walked towards her and stood so close that his clothes brushed hers, blue shirt against white. She could feel his warm breath, his heat…

'I'm not here for long and I've only got sex, and friendship, to offer. I'm not looking for a relationship or commitment or a happy ever after. I just want you in my arms and in my bed.'

'Uh…'

'You interested in hot, slow, crazy sex, Tori? We'd be good together.' Matt dipped his head, placed his mouth on hers and slid his tongue over her bottom lip. Tori made a sound in the back of her throat and gripped the lapels of his jacket with both hands as Matt's hand settled on her hips and yanked her into his hard erection. He teased her lips with his, brushing his expert mouth against hers until her lips parted and his tongue ducked inside. She expected him to push and plunder and was utterly surprised when his mouth slowed down even further and he drugged her with a scorching, slow, sexy kiss.

He sipped and sucked, teased and tormented, keeping the pace slow and subtle, and Tori felt herself squirming against him, her body clamouring for more. Her hands were tangled in his hair at the back of his neck, keeping his mouth on hers, and she wished his hands would do anything but trace small circles on her hips.

Tori yanked her mouth away from his just enough to mutter the word 'more'.

Matt shook his head and stepped back, bringing his hand up to hold the side of her face, his thumb swiping her lower lip. 'No, if I start I can't stop. And when I start I want to know that you are in exactly the same place I am, Tori, looking or fun with no expectations.'

'Um…'

'Have you reached that place?'

'Um…' It seemed to be the only word she could enunciate properly. Matt smiled and stepped back.

'Let me know when you get there.' He picked up his coat and shrugged it on. 'So, do you want the job?'

Tori blinked at the change of subject and it took her a minute to work out what he was talking about, mostly because she was still throbbing Down Town. 'Huh?'

Matt's grin was full and amused. 'Try to keep up, Tori. Do you want the job?'

'Managing Maya's PR? Hell, yes, I want the job.' It took all the will power she had to stop herself from jumping up and throwing her arms around him. Instead she gripped the back of her chair and tried to get her professionalism back. It was really difficult since she could still taste him on her tongue and she felt all turned inside out.

'Good. Let's go home.' Matt took her coat from the coat stand by the door and watched as she shoved her laptop into its case and grabbed her bag.

As she flicked off her monitor her head snapped up. 'Who is she marrying, by the way?' she asked as they walked down the passage to the lifts. Matt pushed the arrow to summon the lift and took her laptop bag from her hand.

'Luke Benson.'

Tori's jaw fell to the floor and Matt had to push her into the lift. Luke Benson, the super-hot, super-successful racing driver. 'Oh, I'm so jealous. When did they meet? How long have they been dating? How did he propose?'

Matt rolled his eyes. 'God, I don't know. Ask Maya in the morning—we're meeting them for breakfast.'

Breakfast with two A-list celebrities, Tori thought, dancing on the spot. Whoot! 'Where we meeting them? At the Connaught or the Savoy?'

They reached the ground floor and Matt pushed her out of the lift again. 'They can't meet publicly, Stripes, remember?'

He'd obviously melted her brains with his kisses. 'Oh, hell, right. So, where, then?'

Matt sent her a wicked smile. 'At the Lancaster Road flat, actually. I'm cooking them breakfast.'

Tori skidded to a stop in the lobby of the building. 'Say what?' she demanded.

'It's the perfect place for us all to meet, especially since neither of them lives in the city. Poppy is working and Alex and Lara are away for the weekend. The flat will be empty and we can talk without being interrupted.'

Tori bit her lip. 'But it's not fancy or smart. It's messy and crazy... It's an old converted fire house, Matt!'

Matt took her arm and pulled her towards the lobby doors and into the freezing, dark November evening. 'It's your house and where I am staying and I love the place. Luke and Maya aren't snobs, Tori, they are just normal people who happen to be rich and successful.'

'Yeah, right,' Tori scoffed, lifting her collar against the cold air seeping down her neck. 'Okay, before I point out that you made all these arrangements without knowing that I'd take the PR job—'

'You would be stupid not to and you are not stupid, Victoria,' Matt said, linking his bare fingers into hers. Tori licked her lips as his warm hand enveloped hers and felt the glow of his compliment warm her from the inside out. 'A little messed up but not stupid.'

'Thanks,' Tori retorted, her tone bone dry. 'But you have one more problem…'

Matt sent her an amused look. 'What?'

'I don't cook.'

Matt laughed, placed a kiss on her temple and his fabulous eyes twinkled. 'That's okay, I do.'

Matt tucked his hands under his armpits and watched as Luke and Maya scrambled into a taxi, both of them flashing him a final smile through the back window before the taxi pulled away into the traffic. He glanced up at the sodden sky and wished for a bit of sun, any sun. Summer would be in full swing back home: scorching days, blue skies and barbecues on the beach.

At least his dad was back at work and back to exercising, Matt thought as he turned around to go back inside, and he seemed to be fully recovered from his bout of pneumonia. He missed him and wished that he were close enough to take him to a pub for a beer, to touch base with him. In the empty hallway downstairs, he yanked out his mobile and his father picked up in two rings.

'Hey, Dad.'

'Matt! How did the breakfast go? Did your PR person deliver?' Matt sat down on the bottom step and grinned at his shoes.

'She delivered. My instincts about her were right, Dad. She might have a crazy personal life but she's as sharp as a tack when it comes to her job. She had a plan of action all drawn up and Maya and Luke like her and, more importantly, seemed to trust her.'

'You've always had good instincts when it comes to people, Matthew. I wish you'd put them to good use and find yourself someone to settle down with.'

'Talking of...'

'You've found someone?' Patrick's voice vibrated with excitement.

'No, jeez, take a breath, old man.' Matt rubbed his forehead with his thumb. 'But Tori and I have this thing cooking and now that she has some distance from her break-up...'

Patrick waited a minute before speaking again. 'Do you think that's a good idea, son? You're going to be working together and you're also living together.'

'Probably not but I've made it pretty clear that this would be a fling until I go.'

'Uh-huh. She agree to this yet?'

'Not exactly. I've thrown it out there. I'm waiting for her to come around.'

'You smooth-talking devil, you,' Patrick said, his voice as dry as the Kalahari Desert. 'One of these days you're going to find a girl and fall in love and I'm going to remind you of this conversation.'

'Still have no plans to do that, Dad. I don't want to—' Matt stopped, not believing that he was about to voice his biggest fear.

'Don't want to what, Matthew?' Patrick gently asked. 'Have someone die on you?'

Matt pulled in a deep breath. 'I don't want to ever miss someone as much as you missed—still miss—Mom.'

Matt clearly heard Patrick's huge sigh. 'This is my journey, Matt, and it won't be yours.'

'Until you can guarantee that I'd rather not take the

chance,' Matt quietly stated before saying goodbye and jogging back up the stairs to his temporary fling.

Because that was all Tori could ever be; it was all any woman could ever be.

Tori was loading the dishwasher when Matt walked back into the kitchen. She took one look at his face and bit her lip. He looked distracted and miles away and Tori felt her stomach roll over. What had she missed? Were they unhappy? Not impressed with her presentation, unhappy with the venue of a country house close to the motor-racing base, didn't they like breakfast? Her? Tori rubbed her hands on her thighs and sent Matt an uncertain look. 'Well?'

Matt handed her a glass and sent her a quizzical look. 'Well, what?'

'Luke and Maya? Happy? Not happy? Are we in business?'

Why was he looking at her as if she'd grown two heads? 'Why wouldn't we be?'

Men! Really! 'Because you are miles away and you looked…distracted. I thought I'd said something you, and they, weren't happy with.'

Matt shook his head. 'No, nothing like that. They love you and love your ideas.'

'I think they just loved your breakfast. Salmon and cream cheese baguettes, fruit salad, poached eggs with hollandaise sauce…made from scratch!' Tori whistled her approval. 'You'll make someone a fantastic wife some day.'

'Haha.' Matt flicked her bottom with the corner of the tea towel.

'Seriously, where did you learn to cook like that?' Tori asked him, slamming the dishwasher door closed and heading for the coffee pot.

'Partly at home and partly because I've always got people in my house and I end up feeding them.' Matt took the coffee cup he held out and pulled out a chair at the kitchen table. 'My clients frequently end up at my house after work and I end up cooking.'

'Why do they come to your house? Why don't they just call you?' Tori asked, sitting opposite him and cradling her cup in her hands. Then she remembered the constant calls to his mobile: some he took; some he ignored. But the damn thing was always ringing. 'Oh, wait, they do call...all the time.'

Matt's shoulder lifted and fell. 'Yep...they call. Often. I've heard every excuse—they want to check a contract clause, need me to explain an endorsement deal—but when you dig deeper it's normally because they are lonely or bored or feeling insecure. They've lost a match, been dumped or had a crappy day, been shouted at by their coach. I'm brother, mother, father, priest, financial advisor, best friend, motivator. I'm usually whatever they need.'

Tori wrinkled her nose. 'So, what you are telling me is that after your long day your clients still end up at your place and emotionally vomit all over you?'

Matt grinned at her turn of phrase. 'Pretty much. That's why I took Isaac's offer to sublet his room. I just wanted a break from them being able to rock up unannounced and demand attention.'

'Pity you can't turn off your phone. I don't blame you for wanting to hide out. Taking care of people is emotionally draining.'

'Actually, I love it and I don't mind that they need me but sometimes I just need a break. And I would love to switch off my phone. But holding their hands, feeding them, counselling them, motivating them, balancing their bank accounts—it's all part of the job.'

'So who is your neediest client?'

Matt grinned. 'Not a chance I'm telling you that.'

Tori smiled. 'It was worth a try.' She tapped her French-manicured nails against the china mug and tipped her head. 'If you are constantly taking care of your clients, who takes care of you?'

There was the two-headed look again. What had she said now that was so left of centre? 'It's not a rocket-scientist question, Matt. Who props you up when you feel blue or flat or exhausted?'

'I—uh—'

Tori kept an enquiring expression on her face and waited for an answer, which Matt eventually, reluctantly, dredged up. 'My dad, I suppose. We connect most days. I talk stuff through with him.'

Okay, that wasn't what she expected to hear. A friend maybe, an ex-girlfriend possibly, but his dad? Jeez, who actually *talked* to their dad these days? 'Seriously? Your dad?'

'Yeah, we're tight. He's smart, funny and he gets me.' Matt leaned back in his chair and stretched out his long, long legs. 'Why are you looking at me like that?'

Tori frowned quickly. 'Sorry, it's just that you talk about your dad as if he's your best mate.'

'He is,' Matt said simply. He sipped his coffee and scratched his jaw. 'Why are you so staggered by this?'

Because it sounded like a fairy tale? Her parents had not been around when she'd been young. Instead she'd had nannies, boarding school and money tossed her way, whereas Matt had grown up in a fully functional, loving relationship with his father.

'I didn't, don't really have parents,' she said quietly. Her mother and father were two fabulously rich but narcissistic individuals who'd separated when she was eleven and spent the rest of her childhood and teenage years arguing about why the *other* parent should be responsible for her.

They'd finally agreed to share custody but neither of

them could be bothered to actually adhere to the ten-minute conversation they'd had about who she should live with. If she was at her mother's, her father forgot to collect her; at her father's and he'd have to track down her mother and demand that she be picked up. Sending her away to Trenton had been the best decision they'd ever made, but then she'd faced the term-end horror show of waiting in the Headmistress's office, surrounded by her luggage, mortified while her parents argued with Miss Sterling about why it wasn't their turn to have her.

How many times had Poppy scooped her up and taken her home because her mother was in St Moritz and refused to come home or her father was in Aspen with his latest snow bunny?

'So were you hatched?' Matt teased.

Tori considered launching into one of her exceptionally funny, self-deprecating stories of her parents' not-so-benign neglect but for once she couldn't be bothered. Or didn't want to. Maybe it had something to do with the straight-up, non-pitying acceptance she saw in his eyes. 'I might as well have been. You know how the saying goes—some people should be tested before being allowed to procreate? My parents were the shining example.'

Matt didn't reply and she was grateful because really silence was the best response to her proclamation. She didn't want to hear platitudes, mock understanding, and empty words. Silence was perfect.

'You're lucky that you have your dad to take care of you, Matt—' She saw his mouth open to instinctively object to the phrase 'take care of' and rolled her eyes. 'Oh, stop being such a macho man. Let me put it in boy-speak—you're lucky to have your dad at your back.'

'Is that what you want, Stripes? Someone to take care of you?' Matt's question came in an even tone, laid-back but still probing. How did he do that?

Tori stared down into her coffee, looking for the words, the phrase, the truth, she'd barely admitted to herself. 'If you asked me that two weeks ago I would've said "hell yes!" but I'm starting to think that maybe, just maybe, I'd like someone just to stand by me while I took care of myself.'

Matt's astounded look—radiating approval—warmed her up from the inside out. He stood up and she was grateful that she was sitting down because she knew that her rapidly dissolving legs wouldn't be able to hold her up. His look was all heat and lust and attraction and all those things that she said she was going to avoid for a while. She licked her lips as he walked around the table, put both his hands under her elbows and yanked her up and into his arms. His body was all hard planes and solid muscle and her hands fisted into his shirt.

With her breasts mashed against his chest, those brilliant eyes glinted down at hers, moving from her mouth to her eyes and back again. Dammit, kiss me already, she thought.

'With pleasure,' Matt murmured.

Did she say that aloud? she briefly wondered before those clever lips covered hers. It didn't matter, she thought, because Matt's mouth was on hers, experienced, seeking. The tip of his tongue pushed between her lips and then he was sliding inside, hot, warm and pushing every nerve ending she possessed into overdrive. She thought she heard Matt groan, felt his fingers dig into the skin on her hip and she lifted one hand to grip the back of his neck, closing her eyes as he left her mouth to trail sweet, slow kisses on the edge of her jaw, across her cheekbone towards her ear. He pulled her ear lobe between his lips, tasting that super-sensitive spot behind her ear.

Dear Lord, he'd done nothing but feed her a couple of hot kisses and her panties were soaking wet and she was considering taking his hand and leading him off to her bed…Izzy's bed, the closest bed.

Tori heard the slam of the front door and, two seconds later, Matt's muttered curse. He stepped back and rubbed the pad of his thumb across her full bottom lip. 'God, you're beautiful,' he murmured. 'I'd like nothing more than to spend the afternoon in bed making love to you…'

'It's not a good idea,' Tori hissed. 'I'm trying to avoid making mistakes with men and I suspect that you would be a big one.'

'And I know that you are high maintenance and I don't do high maintenance.'

'Anyone home?' Poppy's voice drifted through the flat.

'In the kitchen,' Matt called back.

'I am *not* high maintenance,' Tori snapped at Matt as he sat down, no doubt to hide the enormous erection that tented his pants.

'Oh, honey, you define high maintenance,' Matt retorted. 'You need lots of emotional attention and affection and are more difficult and challenging than most woman. You're finicky and demanding, sweet and loyal and you just need to look at me and I'm as hard as a frickin' stone and I… Hi, Poppy. Do you want some breakfast?'

And I what? Tori wanted to demand, her fingers on her lips. What? What? *What?*

Then Matt's mobile rang and he, as per usual, left the room to take a client's call. Give the man a break, Tori wanted to shout at them. It's Saturday, let him have a life!

CHAPTER SEVEN

MATT HIRED AN expensive SUV to get them from Notting Hill to the English country hotel chosen for the press-release weekend. Used to the chaotic traffic in Cape Town and after years of dealing with the erratic driving habits of taxi drivers in his home city, he easily made his way through London and onto the motorway heading north.

He fielded a whole bunch of calls while he was driving and sighed in relief when his mobile finally fell silent. It was a wet, cold, threatening-snow day and Matt adjusted the temperature in the car and sighed at the heat coming up from the seat warmers. He glanced across at Tori, who was unwinding her scarf and unbuttoning her coat. She slipped her arms out of her coat and hung it over the back of her seat and Matt nearly swallowed his tongue as the rich-wine-coloured V-neck sweater pulled across her chest and perfectly delineated her breasts.

Keep looking at those and you're going to end up under a bus, Cross. Literally.

'You warm enough?' he asked, staring hard at the road in front of him.

'Perfect.' She sighed, pulling a cute woollen hat off her head and throwing it onto the back seat. She smiled at him and wiggled down into her seat and interesting things happened in his pants.

'I've hardly seen you all week,' Matt commented.

'We spoke a couple of times every day on the phone,' Tori countered.

'That was work… How are *you*? Has it been as crazy a week for you as it has been for me?'

Tori sighed. 'It's been mad…and I haven't stopped taking calls since we sent the invites to those journos. What's this about? Is Maya retiring? Is she gay? Is she pregnant?'

Matt laughed. 'No connection to Luke?' he asked, signalling so that he could overtake a delivery van.

'Hasn't even blipped on their radar. Men haven't blipped on their radar. Between leaving Drew and falling in love with Luke did she join a nunnery? She hasn't been linked with anyone since Drew.'

Matt twisted his lips. 'She's ultra-picky about her privacy. She and Luke have been very, very circumspect and very few people knew that they were dating, less knew how serious it is between them.'

'Huh. Well, good for them.' Tori half turned in her seat and Matt caught a whiff of her perfume; light, fresh and sexy, dammit. Then again, everything was sexy on her. 'Maya and Luke are not staying at the hotel. They've elected to go home each night…apparently Luke has a place quite close to Silverstone.'

'Mmm.'

'You and I are booked in at the hotel. It's one of those country seventeenth-century homes that have been converted into a boutique hotel. Great food, great ambience…'

'Great sex?' Matt said hopefully, half joking. He slid a look at Tori and couldn't tell what she was thinking by her tipped head and wide eyes. She didn't say anything for a long while and Matt had to work hard to keep his insouciance. He intended to have her in his bed, he thought. She might as well start getting used to the idea.

Tori opened her mouth to speak and Matt held his breath, slightly irked that his heart had sped up in anticipation. His boy was all perky too, hoping to get lucky. 'Why sports management?' Tori asked.

What the hell…? Where was the 'please take me to bed' and the 'can't wait to get you naked too' he expected?

'Sorry, what?'

Tori smiled, the witch, and waved her hand in a slow circle. Her expression suggested that he should start thinking with his big head for a moment. 'Why sports management for a career, Matt?'

Matt sent her another quick look and sighed at the lift of her stubborn chin. Oh, well, talking would make the time go a lot faster than visions of her naked and panting. 'I love sports, being active, and so does my dad. I've always been good at it and planned on making rugby my career. I got pretty far and then didn't make it any further. No matter how hard I trained, how much heart I had, I just couldn't break through that ceiling into the professional leagues.'

Tori curled up in the large seat, her body facing him. Matt down-shifted, hit the accelerator and zoomed past a lorry. Big, fat icy splotches splattered the windscreen and he flicked on his wipers.

'It looks really cold out there,' Tori said. 'Tell me how you made the jump from not being good enough to running what I now realise is one of the premier sports agencies in the world.'

'You Google me, Stripes?'

'I Google everyone. But there's not much personal stuff about you on the web so I have to interrogate you face to face.'

'Ah, old school…I like it.'

Tori folded her arms and waited him out. She wasn't going to let the subject drop, Matt realised. 'I was really down about it until my dad sat me down and said that I could find another way to be involved in sports, with sportsmen. With his guidance I decided to do a psychol-

ogy degree, thinking that I'd go into sports psychology
or coaching. While I was doing that a mate got offered
a place with an English Premier League soccer team...'

'Football...we call it football,' Tori murmured.

'Soccer, football...that sport played by guys who don't
want to get hurt,' Matt quipped. 'I read over his contract,
saw some huge problems and knew right then that I wanted
to be a sports manager.'

'Did you switch your degree to business?'

Matt shook his head. 'Double major, business and psychology. Trust me, I need the psychology degree more than
the business degree.'

'Why?'

Matt lifted a shoulder. 'As I said to you the other day,
my clients can be quite needy.'

'Judging by the amount of calls you receive and the
counselling you do they are demanding, attention seeking,
frequently crazy and insecure. Give them a swift kick up
their jack and send them on their way.'

Matt grinned. 'Don't give up your day job, Tori.'

She sighed. 'Sometimes the only way people see the
light is when they are smacked on the head with a ten-
pound hammer.'

'Was catching what's his face in bed with the crazy
fairy your ten-pound-hammer equivalent?'

'Oh, yes.' Tori nodded, looking down at her hands.
'Though to be fair, life did smack me on the head a couple of times before that to get my attention.'

'Spill.'

'I knew, deep inside, that he was cheating on me but I
didn't want to admit it to myself. The wearing-my-under-
wear episode was a fairly big clue that his lift didn't go
to the top floor.'

Matt's jaw dropped open. 'He tried on your underwear?'

'Mmm. Bizarre much?'

'Very.' Matt dropped his hand onto her knee that was covered in opaque black tights. Knee boots covered her lower legs and a snug black skirt stopped a couple of inches above her knee. 'For the record, the only way I'll only enjoy your lingerie, which, I have to say, is freaking hot, is by removing it inch by inch.'

Tori frowned. 'How would you know if my underwear is hot?'

'I live in a house with three women and there is always a piece of underwear in the bathroom, either hanging on a towel rail or left on the floor. All silky, all sexy and all Lara's work, I presume?'

'You presume right.'

'Ergo…freaking hot.'

Tori fought a grin and lifted her nose. 'I'll concede the point. My underwear is freaking hot.'

Matt wanted to thunk his forehead against the wheel but in the interest of not getting…well, dead…he resisted. He couldn't help noticing that Tori didn't comment on whether he would be removing her clothing in the foreseeable future or not. He had a vested interest in finding out what her position was on said undergarment removal.

'Exit in two hundred yards…' The GPS intoned in a Margaret Thatcher voice.

After all, he'd spent an enormous amount of time fantasising about how exactly said removal would take place. A strap sliding down her arm, a finger hooking down a demi-cup—that was one of those sexy half-cup bras, wasn't it?—to reveal a rosy nipple…

'Exit in one hundred yards…'

He'd tongue that exposed nipple, long sexy slides while letting the silk, satin, lace rub his chin, his cheek…

'Exit now, exit now…'

Matt flew past the exit, glanced at the GPS and swore. How the hell did he miss the exit?

'Why didn't you warn me?' he demanded, looking in his rear-view mirror as their turn-off faded in the gloom.

'Actually, I thought that the three warnings from the GPS were enough. You were miles away. What on earth were you thinking about?'

'Your nipples.'

'Excuse me?'

'I was having a little fantasy about your sexy lingerie and your boobs.' Matt glanced at the GPS again. 'Okay, so next exit and we add on a half-hour to our journey.'

Tori shook her head. 'Next exit and I'll show you a quick way to get there.'

'You familiar with this part of the country?' Matt asked.

'Sure, very familiar with the country hotel we're staying at too,' Tori said on a wistful sigh. 'It was my maternal grandparents' house, now run by my cousin Colin and his business partner and lover, Brett. Our grandparents are still hanging around, as batty as fruit cakes but, lucky you, they are away until Sunday. Lucky because they refuse to accept that Colin is running a hotel and they like to pretend that the guests are their guests...so they automatically feed them alcohol and dirty jokes. They would also automatically assume we are lovers and would make an effort to embarrass me as much as possible.'

Matt shot her a hot look.

'Okay, let me get this straight. We are staying in and holding one of the most important press conferences this year at a country hotel that belongs to your family and your crazy grandparents will get everyone liquored as soon as possible?' Matt tasted panic at the back of his throat and thought that he'd made a colossal mistake. 'On what planet did you think this was a good idea, Tori?'

'Cool your jets, Cross. Ridley Hall is consistently rated as the best country hotel in the country and the food is sublime and the guests adore the wrinklies. Guests feel cheated if they don't engage with Lady and Lord Ridley and didn't you hear the part about them being away? And Colin runs a tight ship and he'll also keep the vultures on time and moving them along. I've discussed this with him and he's got our back.'

Matt frowned. 'You told him about Maya and Luke?'

'Didn't have to,' Tori answered smugly. 'He's known about them for ages. Romantic dinners, overnight stays, weekends.'

'And he hasn't spilt the beans? Impressive.' Matt whistled.

'Oh, he's had bigger fish than Maya and Luke snuggling up beneath his sheets. Married and sneaking away for a dirty weekend, married and sneaking away for a dirty weekend with your lover, married and sneaking away with your lover of the same sex—Colin has seen it all. He could've retired on the money the tabloids paid him for info. That's why he doesn't allow any members of the press to sleep on the premises...ever. He has a reputation for being the soul of discretion and intends to keep that rep.' Tori's voice had turned tart midway through that spiel and Matt didn't need to look at her to see that she was narked. 'Did you really think that I would jeopardise this job by holding the press conference somewhere that I didn't have a hundred per cent confidence in?'

'Uh...sorry?'

'You should be,' Tori muttered before telling him to take the next exit.

After a minute's silence, Matt glanced at her again. 'Can I go back to fantasising about your boobs now?'

Matt didn't need to be looking at Tori to know that she rolled her eyes at him. 'Which is your way of getting me to answer whether I'm going to sleep with you or not.'

Matt waited a beat. 'Well, are you?'

Tori yanked a bottle of water from the cup holder,

cracked the seal and took a long swallow. After she re-capped the bottle, she pushed her hair behind her ears and turned to look at him. Matt took his eyes off the road long enough to raise an enquiring eyebrow at her.

'I don't understand you...' she said in a quick, jerky voice. 'I've thrown myself at you twice and both times you kicked me into touch. Then I back off and then you want me. Is this about the chase or is something else going on that I don't know about?'

Matt waited a beat before answering. 'You...you're different.'

'How?' Tori demanded.

'Well, for one thing, I can see that you are fully over that idiot ex of yours and you haven't wasted any more tears over him. For another, I think you need a guy to show you how you should be treated.'

'Excuse me?' Tori yelped and in the same breath told him to turn left at the T-junction.

Matt took the turn and wondered whether he was doing the right thing, whether he was about to say the right thing. 'Tori, from the little I have gathered about you, I think that you've settled for men that really aren't good enough for you.'

'That's word for word Poppy coming out of your mouth,' Tori muttered.

Busted, Matt thought, and decided the best way forward was to be honest. 'I'm really attracted to you and I know you are attracted to me. I'm here until month end, and I'd like to spend that time with you, with the full understanding that I will leave and that there won't be any type of relationship after I've gone. Not infrequent, not long term, nothing.'

Matt continued. 'Look, for the duration of the month, this fling, I promise that we'll have fun, lots of great sex, and I'll treat you like you should be treated.'

'And how is that?' Tori asked softly.

'Like you are incredibly special, and maybe the next time you won't settle for anything less from a man than what you deserve,' Matt replied in his most serious voice. Because she did deserve that, he thought. Every woman deserved that.

'So, Stripes, what do you think?'

'The turn-off to Ridley Hall is coming up on your right,' Tori replied.

'I meant, what do you think about having a fling? With me?' Matt demanded, swinging into the driveway that was lined with oak trees. The magnificent trees were devoid of leaves now but in the summer they would be magnificent, Matt thought, with the tiny fragment of his brain that wasn't occupied with wondering if he was going to get lucky tonight.

'I'll think about it,' Tori said. 'Oh, look! There's Colin!'

She'll think about it? Matt scowled. Seriously? And how long did said thinking take?

Tori kissed and hugged her cousin hello, popped her head into the kitchen to do the same to Brett, his partner and the best chef she knew. She tasted his French onion soup, proclaimed it delicious and wandered back into the huge hall where Colin was standing beside her small suitcase. She looked around for Matt and saw that he'd headed into the main lounge to take a call. Of course. What else would he be doing?

'I'll walk you upstairs and see that you get settled in,' Colin told her, gripping her case by its handle.

'Col, I'm fine. I always sleep in the Daisy room and I can find it in my sleep. I only spent large portions of my childhood here,' Tori muttered, trying to tug the bag out of his grasp.

'Stop being a pain and let's go. I want to gossip about that hunky man in my hall!' Colin hissed.

Tori let go of the bag and followed Colin up the impressive staircase, past six-foot-high portraits of Ridley ancestors—she always expected them to start whispering to her, like the portraits at Hogwarts. However, sadly, it had yet to happen.

'He is my client and Maya Bennet's manager. He hired me to run the PR for this horse and pony show.'

'And why wouldn't he?' Colin demanded as they reached the top of the stairs. 'You're fantastic at your job.'

And that was why Colin was her favourite cousin, the closest thing she had to a brother, or, come to think of it, sister. As two lonely and rejected only children, they'd banded together as children and their love and loyalty to each other had extended into adulthood. 'Heard from your mum?' Tori quietly asked.

'No, heard from yours?'

Tori shook her head. Their mothers were sisters, equally spoilt and equally uninterested in their children. Peas in a pod, Tori thought, linking her hand in his and laying her head on his arm.

'So tell me about Mr Tight Buns.' Colin ordered.

'Matt wants to have an affair with me. A brief, glorious, brilliant affair that has a shelf life.'

Colin lifted his eyebrows as he opened the door to the Daisy room, so called because of the white bedding with daisy yellow and black accents. Tori briefly wondered where Matt was sleeping: in the Tulip room that had an inter-connecting door to hers or in the more masculine Orchid room of deep purples and blues?

'I can move him to the Tulip room if that's what you want,' Colin said, reading her mind. He grinned at her as he placed her bag on the small table and deftly unzipped it. He shook his head at her messy packing and immediately started unpacking her clothes. Tori lay back on the king-size canopied bed and kicked off her shoes. 'What do you think I should do, Col?'

'I don't know…what do you think you should do?'

Colin walked across to her and placed both hands on her shoulders and looked down into her upturned face. 'He's not offering you love, right?'

'Right.'

'Or commitment.'

'Right. But he'll show me how I should be treated.'

'Mmm. So, he's been upfront and honest?'

'Yes, he has.' Tori nodded.

'So, let me see if I've got this right. A fantastic-looking man is offering you a fun time with no commitment for a couple of weeks and you are hesitating? Honey, what is wrong with you? You hopped into a relationship with the D-bag after a week and he was mutated from shower mould.'

Tori flopped backwards on the bed. 'Make the decision for me, Colin, so that I can blame you later.'

Colin crawled up onto the bed next to her, kissed her nose and crawled back. 'Sure. Have a fling with Matt of the Mighty Cute Ass. Blame me later…now carry on with your own unpacking! Jeez, anyone would think that you expect to be treated like a guest!'

Colin just laughed when a very expensive silk pillow flew past his head and landed in the hall.

Guests were expected to dress for dinner at Ridley Hall, or, at the very least, they were expected to change. Knowing that she'd get a mouthful from her cousin if she didn't at least appear to make an effort, Tori changed into black woollen pants and a thick Aran sweater. She knew that Col had upgraded the central heating and the bedrooms were toasty warm but it was fairly difficult to heat the enormous dining room and main reception rooms and she had no wish to masquerade as a human popsicle for the next few hours. Country chic, she thought, checking her reflection in the free-standing antique mirror, but she would probably still not be appropriately dressed for dinner.

Colin, and her grandmother—absent or not—expected nothing less than a cocktail dress, stilettos and chandelier-sized earrings. The fact that Stella frequently arrived to dinner in muddy jodhpurs and mucky riding boots—but always wearing bright red lipstick—was beside the point. Stella was very much a do-as-I-say-and-not-as-I-do type of grandmother.

Thinking that she should warn Matt to dress warm, she stopped at the door to the Orchid room and banged on his door. Not hearing movement inside, she wondered if he'd gone down to dinner without her and frowned. She knocked again and, when he didn't reply, opened the door and peeked in. The door to the bathroom was half closed and she could hear the steady beat of the shower and a vision of a naked Matt popped into her head. Long, lean muscles, ridged stomach, that tanned back and the paler flesh of his buttocks. The perfect T of hair that narrowed down into a thick thatch of black hair, his penis large and rock-hard.

She was thrumming at the thought of all that hard, fragrant-with-soap male flesh just waiting to be touched, explored by her hands, her mouth, licked and stroked by her tongue. Tori reached out and gripped the back of a wingback chair to give her knees some support, something to hold onto so that she didn't gallop her way into the bathroom and start having her way with him.

She was taking a break from jumping into quick relationships with men, she told herself.

It's for a few weeks and it's just about sex, her libido replied. He can't give you the love that you're looking for, but he can give you what you want: sex. You just have to say the word.

I'm trying to be smart…

You have never been smart with men—why start now?

Dear God. Tori whimpered aloud. I really, really want to join him in that shower.

Tori's head snapped up as the door to the bathroom was yanked open and Matt stepped out, a towel wrapped around his waist and droplets of water still on his chest and arms. His eyes widened in surprise at seeing her in his room. 'Hi, how long have you…?'

He saw something on her face that dried up his words—probably the 'take me now' sign that was flashing from her eyes—and he crossed the room to her, his big hands lifting to hold her face, his mouth descending to cover hers. At the first touch of his lips, her mouth softened, opened and let him in.

She dimly felt him drop his hands to pull hers off the chair and to hold them against his chest, flattening them out so that her fingers were flat against his pecs, his flesh wet and warm beneath her palms. His mouth nibbled and suckled and teased and she followed where he led, knowing that no one had ever pulled her so thoroughly out of herself as he did with one devastating kiss.

Matt's hand burrowed under her jersey and pulled her silk T-shirt out from her pants and his warm hand slid up her side, his thumb brushing the underside of her breast, running over her bra strap and down to her hip again. Tori murmured insensible words of encouragement, silently demanding him to touch her. His thumb finally brushed her nipple as he feathered kisses along her jaw.

'More, more, more,' Tori chanted softly, stepping away from him and lifting her jersey and T-shirt in one fluid movement, revealing a lilac lace bra covering her aching pointed nipples.

Matt stared at her chest and folded his arms, sucking in his sexy bottom lip. 'Take your bra off, Tori,' he commanded. 'I need to see you.'

Tori placed her hands behind her back and flipped open the snap, holding her arms against her sides to keep the bra in place. 'Drop it,' Matt demanded, his fingers digging into the muscles of his opposite arm. Tori knew that he was struggling to keep himself from reaching for her, astounded by the heat and passion in his now jade-green eyes.

Tori pulled her bra off and let it flutter to the floor. She saw his Adam's apple bob and, enjoying his attention, she shook her head when he looked as if he was about to step towards her. Turning half away from him, she deliberately bent over and gave him a view of her bottom as she pulled the short zip of her boots down and slipped them off her feet. Shoeless and an inch shorter, she looked over her shoulder and saw that Matt was looking at her ass; no, looking was too tame a word. Gaping? Gawking? Ogling? She whipped her head back around and smiled at the floor. Unzipping her pants, she hooked her thumbs into the band and slowly, ever so slowly, shimmied the material down her hips, revealing the thin cord of a tiny thong that lay between her butt cheeks.

'You're killing me, woman,' Matt muttered and that was the only warning she got before a strong arm banded around her stomach and she was easily lifted and deposited face down onto the massive bed behind her.

His mobile rang and she scowled. 'You'd better not be thinking of getting that, Cross.'

'Not a chance in hell. Give me a sec to switch it off.' Matt fiddled with his phone before rolling her over and, instead of kissing her or touching her, he let his eyes travel from her face down her length to her pink-tipped toes.

'You are far better than I remember, Victoria, and I

have a very good memory,' Matt growled. He lay on his side next to her, his head in the palm of his hand. 'You sure you want to do this?'

Tori somehow managed to make her head move up and down.

'Good, because I intend to rock your world.' Matt's thumb whispered across her cheekbone. 'Slowly and very thoroughly.'

Tori gulped and then sighed as Matt's head lowered and his amazing mouth went to work. This was kissing, Tori thought, with no beginning and no ending. Sexy, sure, casual nips and deep forays, wet slides followed by teasing sucks. His hands were equally deft: hot strokes down her back, over her hip, across her stomach. His hand moved up to cover her breast and he rubbed the centre of his palm across her nipple, then pulled it into a harder peak before dropping his head and laving it with his tongue.

No part of her body was left untouched: her belly button was explored and tasted, her inner thighs sampled, the backs of her knees tickled. He spent some time exploring each knob of her spine, kneading her bum before his fingers delved behind her and found her soaking wet and fire-hot.

Matt pulled his hand out from under her and kissed her deeply as one finger slipped inside her and then two. His thumb flicked her and she keened out, lifting her hips to take him deeper, whimpering into his mouth to give her more. Matt rolled away and pulled out the drawer of the bedside table and cursed when the drawer fell to the floor and his wallet, mobile, e-reader and box of condoms scattered across the carpet. Leaning down, he reached for the condoms, ripped the box open and scattered foil packets over the bed. He ripped the top of one off with his teeth, yanked his towel away and batted Tori's hands away when she tried to help him.

'If you touch me I'm going to explode,' he muttered as the latex rolled down him.

'Hurry,' Tori instructed, her hand between her legs.

Matt pulled her hand away. 'That's my job.' He growled and replaced her fingers with his, testing her readiness. 'You're so hot and so wet. You ready for me, Stripes?'

'Hurry. Up,' Tori responded through gritted teeth. 'How do you want to do this?'

Matt flicked her an impatient glance. 'Huh?'

'Doggy? The Afternoon Delight? The Sphinx?'

Matt shook his head. 'How about straight-up missionary so that I can see your eyes cross when I slide into you?' Matt suggested as he positioned himself over her.

'Straight-up missionary works for me.' Tori sighed happily and whimpered when the tip of his penis brushed against her clitoris. 'That feels so good—you feel so good.'

'Then this will feel better,' Matt promised and slid into her with one sure slide, groaning deeply as he buried himself inside her.

Tori whimpered, arched up, ground her hips against him and came instantly and wildly, her body splintering into a million fragments. She pumped her hips like a crazy woman, wanting more of the indescribable pleasure, and felt herself build again. Matt's hands slid under her to anchor her as he pounded into her and every stroke lifted her higher, pushing her closer to that beautiful edge she couldn't wait to tumble from again.

'Tori,' Matt commanded. 'Look at me. Open your eyes.'

Tori fluttered her eyes open and squeezed them shut when Matt rotated his hips and hit another spot deep inside her that had been neglected up until now. Stars danced behind her eyes.

'Look at me. I want to see you when you come.'

Tori forced her eyelids to separate and as soon as her eyes connected with Matt's he drove hard and deep and she tumbled over the edge, her body fragmenting with inexpressible pleasure. She felt Matt shudder, heard his groan and buried her fingers into his hip bones as he pulsed inside her, muttering unintelligible words in her ear.

Tori's first thought, as her heart rate slowed and the world started to make sense again, was that she'd forgotten how damn wonderful missionary sex could be.

CHAPTER EIGHT

DESPITE A FAIR bit of experience with the opposite sex, Tori didn't really know what to say to a man she barely knew and with whom she'd shared mind-blowing sex.

Thanks bunches.

You are a sex god.

Do me again. And again. And again...

Tori felt Matt roll away and watched as he walked around the bed, utterly at ease, and headed back towards the bathroom. She heard the toilet flush and thought that she should make the effort to get up; instead she just flipped the edge of the royal-purple bedspread over her and rolled onto her side, tucking her hands under the pillow.

She'd never been taken like that, Tori thought. Making love to Matt had been raw, sensual, down-to-her-toes sexy... It had been a real out-of-body experience and she'd loved every minute of it. She could have this, with him, for another few weeks, she thought. She could have the sensual experience of pleasuring and being pleasured by him and enjoy this sex-based friendship without any expectations or complications.

He would treat her as she deserved to be treated... Those words alone had her trembling. What would that be like? What would being the focus of the attention of this amazingly smart and handsome, nice man be like? She needed to find out— She'd always tried too hard and sacrificed too much for the men in her life and she felt she deserved, no, needed, to have the tables flipped.

Except that it made her feel damn uncomfortable.

She wasn't sure how this brief fling was supposed to work because she'd never had one before. She didn't do no-strings attached—hell, all her relationships had had so many strings they could have anchored a hot-air balloon. She went into relationships with expectations of love and romance and happily ever after; she didn't know how to not get attached. How could she remain disconnected yet intimate? And she didn't care what anyone said, having someone inside you giving you pleasure was as intimate as two people could get!

Disconnected yet intimate…could she walk this tight-rope?

Tori watched as Matt walked towards her from the bathroom, still naked and still marginally happy to see her. He sat on the edge of the bed next to her and picked a strand of hair off her cheek and tucked it behind her ear.

'You okay?' he asked, in his deep voice.

Tori nodded.

'You sure?'

'Very. Thanks, it was…' Tori couldn't find the word she was looking for and found and used 'great'. Dork word, she thought.

'It was…great.' Matt's mouth twitched as he repeated the word. 'And it will get greater.' He rested his hand on her hip and she could feel his heat through the fabric. 'So, let's talk about the purple mammoth in the room. Do you want to do this some more or is this a one-time thing?'

Tori made herself speak. 'More, please.'

'OK…I would be happier if you said that with a great deal more enthusiasm,' Matt stated, stroking her arm from her shoulder to her wrist. 'What's the problem, Tori?'

Tori sat up, hiked the bedspread up under her arms and pursed her lips. 'I don't know how to do this.'

Matt looked from her to the bed. 'You more than knew what you were doing, Stripes. Didn't my inability to talk clue you in?'

Tori bit her bottom lip and dismissed his teasing with a toss of her head. 'I don't know the rules of this fling, Matt. How does it work?'

Matt rubbed his jaw and tried, unsuccessfully, to hide his grin. 'Uh…rules?'

Tori gritted her teeth. 'Look, if you're not going to take this seriously—'

'Whoah!' Matt lifted a hand in peace. 'You really want some rules, huh?'

Tori plucked the fabric on the bed between her forefinger and thumb. 'Maybe rules is the wrong word—guidelines would be better. I mean, how many times do you want us to meet a week? Do you want anything…um…odd? I need to know before I say yes so that I can say no, now. Are we going to tell our friends that we are doing this or do we keep it quiet?'

Matt looked at her, absolutely astonished, and eventually shook his head. 'Holy crap, Tori, what kind of clowns have you been dating?' He didn't wait for her to answer and continued speaking. 'There's only one rule and it's non-negotiable. We don't bed-hop.'

'Bed-hop?'

'For the duration that we are together, we are together. We only sleep with each other.'

Tori blinked at him. 'Obviously. Anything else would be…ick.'

Matt let out a relieved sigh. 'Okay, then…good. As for the number of times a week? Once? Every day? Twice on Tuesdays and none on Thursdays? Honey, I don't know because I don't know what sort of mood you, or I, will be in, that day. You might have a headache or I might have had a craptastic day and just feel like getting hammered with Alex or Isaac or one of my clients. If we want to hook up and the other doesn't, it's a simple no and no hard feelings.'

Oh. Okay, Tori thought. Phew.

'As for the odd stuff…what constitutes odd? In my book oral sex isn't odd, whips and chains and weird clothing is.'

'Threesomes?' Tori held her breath.

'A fantasy and not something I will be asking of you.' Matt held Tori's eyes. 'One more thing and if you don't believe anything else I tell you, then believe this, Victoria: no is non-negotiable. I do the smallest thing you don't like and you say no and that's it, I don't do it again. You are in the driving seat sex-wise. If you're not a thousand per cent comfortable then I suck as a lover.'

Wow, Tori thought, staring at him, her mouth slightly open. Double, triple wow!

'As for letting our friends know…why don't we play that by ear?' Matt suggested.

Tori nodded. 'Okay, we can do that.'

'Anything else, my little worry wart? Because we're already late for dinner.'

Tori allowed the bedspread to drop and smiled smugly when Matt's eyes dropped to her chest and his hand reached out to hold her breast, his thumb rubbing her already hard nipple. 'What say we skip dinner and raid the kitchen later?'

'Why? And what on earth are we going to do instead?' Matt teased.

Tori climbed up onto her knees, pushed Matt back onto the bed and straddled his hips. 'I'm sure we can find something to occupy us…'

Matt, lying on his stomach, forced his eyes open and turned his head and squinted at the acre of purple bedding next to him. Huh, no warm female flesh in the immediate vicinity. Dammit, since he had an excellent morning erection that he thought Tori would appreciate. Yawning, he lifted his wrist and looked at the face of his watch—it was half-seven and today was the big announcement day.

Frankly he'd rather stay in bed with Tori and spend some more time with her delectable body than watch the media super-storm that Maya and Luke's engagement would unleash.

Where was Tori anyway? Matt wondered, rolling over and sitting up. He rubbed the sleep out of his eyes and took a moment to visualise the day. The press were due to arrive at nine-thirty and the announcement would be made in the adjoining mini conference and function room behind Ridley Hall at ten. Following that Maya and Luke would pose for photographs and had agreed to a series of fifteen-minute interviews, either as a couple or alone.

Longer, more in-depth interviews were scheduled for the next morning, Sunday, and then they would leave Ridley Hall and the country for a week's break in the Turks and Caicos. He'd do anything for some sun; he was sick of these dank and dismal days and was even considering undertaking the twelve-hour flight home for a long weekend so that he could stock up on his Vitamin D.

But that would mean four or five days away from Tori and that wasn't something he wanted to contemplate since he only had a short time with her. Matt swung his legs over the side of the bed and sat on the edge, staring down at the plush carpet below his feet.

She'd surprised him last night with her reaction to his offer of a no-strings affair. He'd expected her to be a lot more sophisticated in her reaction and a great deal more confident. It was hard to reconcile her flirty, breezy, woman-of-the-world façade with the hesitant woman from the night before. She looked younger than she appeared and a lot more vulnerable...

Matt scrubbed his face with his hands. Hell, he hoped he wasn't making a mistake with her; he knew that she normally went into relationships looking for love and commitment and, while she said that she understood that he had none of that to give, he hoped she meant it.

He didn't want her to expect more from him than what he could give, which was essentially everything physical and nothing emotional. He liked her, so spending time with her outside the bedroom wouldn't be hard, but he hoped she didn't expect more, feel more.

He really didn't want her to get hurt... He suspected that Tori had been hurt enough by members of his sex.

Talking of, where was the woman...?

Matt yanked on a pair of jeans and pulled on a sweatshirt and walked out of the room. He ambled towards the room that Tori had been allocated and smiled at the feminine stream of curses that drifted over to him through the half-open door. Nudging the door open with his foot, he lifted his eyebrows at the chaos within. It looked as if the women's department of an upmarket store had vomited its inventory into the room. How the hell had Tori managed to fit so many items into that reasonably small suitcase?

And why?

Matt leaned his shoulder into the door jamb of her room and watched as she picked up a pair of trousers and placed them on the bed between the lapels of a purple suede jacket. She shook her head in disgust, picked up the trousers and tossed them to one side.

Then she picked up a black dress and held it against her slight frame, frowning at herself in the free-standing mirror.

'What'cha doing?' he asked, jamming his hands into the pockets of his Levi's.

Tori whirled around and slapped her hands onto her hips, which just highlighted their slimness covered by cream-coloured boy-cut panties. A short T-shirt flirted with the top band of those panties and her breasts were unrestrained by a bra. Matt felt the saliva in his mouth disappear and felt the tightening of his pants. 'It's about time you woke up. The press conference is soon and I have to read out Maya and Luke's statement and I have nothing to wear!'

Matt twisted his lips. 'Stripes, you have an entire collection in this room.'

'But nothing is working! I need to look chic but accessible, professional but warm! And my hair is a mess and I have a spot on my chin and I need to shower!'

High maintenance, Matt thought with a smile. Finicky, perfectionistic, slightly crazy. Why did he find all that so damn attractive?

Tori shoved her fingers into her hair and tugged. 'Aarrrgh! I think I am going to throw up. I need to check the press release—'

Matt grinned as he stood up and walked into the room, stepping over shoes on his way to her. 'We did that yesterday.'

'I need to check the conference room, the press kits.'

When he reached her, Matt gripped the side of her face and tipped her head up. 'Colin will do that. You need to take a deep breath and after that you need coffee—or a sedative. And you need to kiss me good morning.'

Tori bit her lip. 'No time—'

Matt dipped his head and nibbled the side of her neck. 'There's always time to be kissed, Victoria.'

'Seriously, Matt—' Tori muttered and Matt smiled when she lifted her chin and angled her head to give him better access.

'Good morning, Tori.' Matt spoke the words against her skin. 'Black trousers, black T-shirt, purple jacket. Those kick-ass boots.'

He moved onto her cheekbone, feathering kisses along that gorgeous ridge while his hands came up to cup her breasts. Tori, her eyes bluer with passion, pulled her head away and blinked at him.

'What?'

'I'm making an executive decision about your outfit,' Matt informed her, putting his hands below her bottom and hoisting her up. Tori's legs automatically wrapped around and gripped his hips, her mound riding his now hard-as-concrete erection. 'That'll save you a half-hour.'

Tori draped her arms over his shoulders. 'I don't have time to play with you, Matt.'

Matt ignored her as he walked backwards to the bed, whipping her around as the backs of his knees hit the bed and dumping her on top of a pile of clothes.

'Matt, I need to make sure everything is perfect. I can't mess this up. It's too important. I don't want to let anyone down.'

And didn't that say so much about her? Matt thought. He caught the vulnerability and fear in her eyes and ran a reassuring hand down her arm. 'You won't. It will be fine; you'll be fine. You just need to relax and I have the perfect solution…'

On Sunday afternoon Tori stood at the tall windows of the main lounge in Ridley Hall and watched as the sedan circled the rose garden in front of Ridley Hall and disappeared down the driveway.

She laid her forehead against the glass pane and placed her hands on either side of her head. The last journalist was gone, Maya and Luke's engagement had made the papers that morning and the last of the in-depth interviews were done.

She'd pulled it off. Now she needed a drink and twelve hours of solid sleep; she was exhausted. She'd been run off her feet all day yesterday, co-ordinating photo shoots and interviews, and when she'd finally got to bed she'd found that playing with Matt's hard body was far more fun than sleeping. No wonder she felt like a zombie in a horror movie.

'Coffee?' Matt asked from behind her.

'God, yes.' Tori's breath fogged up the glass and she drew a heart in it with her index finger before turning around and walking over to him to take the cup he held out.

She sat down on a burgundy and silver striped chair and crossed her legs and nibbled on her bottom lip. 'You happy?'

Matt, dressed in jeans and a cream jersey that fell in a straight line to his hips, raised a black brow. 'About what?'

'This weekend, you twit. Work. The fact that you don't let me get any sleep tells me that you are quite happy with how we play.'

Matt stretched his long legs out and linked his hands behind his head. The muscles bunching tightened the fabric of his jersey around his arms and she felt sparks shoot down from her belly button to her happy place. Matt just had to breathe to turn her on.

'I am very happy with how we play,' Matt drawled. 'As for your work…'

Tori leaned forward, balancing her cup on her knee, and told herself that she knew she'd done well, that the entire process had run smoothly, that Maya and Luke were impressed and that she didn't need Matt's approval, his compliments.

She did need him though, she thought. She needed him to realise that she was more than a pretty face, a drama

queen, a good lay. She'd like his respect, his approval…
She'd like him to like her. Not lust after her, *like* her.

Because she liked him, probably more than she should.

'As for my work…' she prompted. Just get with it already,
she silently begged him.

Matt dropped his arms and sat up, his eyes sombre and
serious. 'You're damn good at what you do, Tori. You're
organised and efficient and you're nobody's pushover.
Good job.'

Tori let out a long breath. That! That was what she lived
for: affirmation, praise, and confirmation that she was
more than just a pretty face. That she had a brain and drive
and ambition. And when it came from a man she liked,
who had a steel-trap mind under that easy-going façade,
it meant that much more.

Because when last had she had a man in her life who
respected her? That would be never…

'It shouldn't matter,' Matt said quietly.

'What?'

'What I think shouldn't matter,' Matt stated. 'You know
that you did everything that was expected of you and you
did it with aplomb. You should trust yourself more, Tori,
have more confidence.'

Tori, very gently, placed her half-full coffee cup on the
table between them. 'You are my client. I wanted to make
sure that you were satisfied.'

'You don't know me that well but you should know that
if I wasn't then I would've told you a lot earlier than this.'

'I was just checking.' Tori pushed her hair behind her
ears. 'You're just so laid-back…'

'Not when it comes to business and that's a cop out.'
Matt touched his ears. 'You always do that—push your
hair back, when you are nervous, when you've been caught

out. You weren't just checking. You need verbal affirmation. Why?'

Because I never got any, ever? Because her parents, when they could be bothered to talk to her, were either uninterested in her and her life or critical? Because she could never remember a 'well done', a 'good job', a 'proud of you'. Was it so wrong to still want that, need that?

And why did Matt always have to call her on her foibles? Why couldn't he just leave it alone without psychoanalysing her, without playing life coach? And surely this wasn't the conversation that people in a no-strings-attached thing should have? It was a little too uncomfortable, too deep.

Tori lifted her chin. 'Put your psychology degree away, Dr Freud. I'm too tired to be on your couch today.'

Matt cocked his head. 'Pity, because I thought we could finally put work away and you could come over here and we could neck.'

Tori felt the familiar humming of her nerve endings on fire and arched a brow. 'Just neck?'

Matt twisted his lips. 'Yeah, unfortunately.'

'You too tired?' Tori asked, standing up and walking around the table to stand in front of him.

Matt's hands settled on her hips and he dropped his forehead to her flat stomach. 'Nope. We're out of condoms. If I take you upstairs we might end up having a very big problem in nine months' time.'

'In that case, let's stay down here and just neck,' Tori agreed, dropping into his lap.

Matt nuzzled her jaw, his two-day-old scruff rubbing her skin. 'Thought you'd see it my way.'

They were approaching the outskirts of London when Tori's mobile buzzed and Tori held it to her ear. Above the music playing softly Matt could hear the deep rumble of a male voice that he recognised as Alex's.

As he tuned her banter out he realised that he was exhausted. Sleep had been sacrificed for phenomenal sex and it was a sacrifice he was happy to make. Any day or time of the week. Hey, he was a guy—he'd forgo practically anything for sex.

Sleeping with Tori had been…strange, he thought. Not strange as in weird or creepy but strange as in…unlike any sex that he'd had before. It had been hot and steamy but also…sweet. Maybe sweet wasn't the right word, neither was innocent, although there had been a quality of innocence about Tori's lovemaking. With her history of torrid relationships and the fact that her ex had liked pushing the boundaries—he was never, ever going to ask for details!—he was surprised that Tori came across as ingenuous and anxious to please.

Then again, he was learning that, under her slick and sassy exterior, Tori's actual default setting was redlining in 'anxious to please' and 'please like me'. He spent his life bolstering his clients so doing the same for her should annoy him but, very strangely, it didn't.

She was such an odd, intriguing combination of fearless and frightened, confident and crazy. He hadn't nearly had enough of her yet…

'That was Alex,' Tori said, dropping her mobile into her lap. 'Checking in.'

'You have a good group of friends—they adore you.'

Tori thunked her head back against the headrest and wrinkled her nose. 'That they do. It was nice of them…and you…to allow me to move back in after I left Mark, even if I have to sleep on the ironing-board bed in the coffin.'

'Drama queen,' he gently teased.

'Says the man sleeping in an enormous, soft bed,' Tori retorted.

He shouldn't, he really shouldn't… He should be the sensible one and keep the boundaries defined between them. Inviting her to share his room while he was staying in London was exactly opposite of what he intended to do with Tori; they were going to hang out, have some great sex and then they'd be able to retreat to their respective spaces. Alone. That way they'd keep reminding themselves that this relationship had an expiry date, that it couldn't go anywhere.

It would keep them—her, mostly—from doing something stupid like getting involved, from feeling anything more than lust…

He knew what it felt like when you paid the ultimate price for losing what you loved…

On the other hand, it was stupid and insulting to send her back to her coffin after he'd made love to her. It would be rude, as well. And he'd never get any sleep thinking of her downstairs, so uncomfortable…

'Move into my room with me.' The words tumbled out of his mouth.

Tori flicked him an astounded look out of her bold blue eyes. 'Uh…I don't think that's a good idea.'

'I know it's not but if we are going to be together then we need a bed and if we try to make love in your rabbit hutch, we'll break the bed and or do ourselves some damage.'

Tori bit her lip and stared out of the window. 'I still don't think it's smart. I'm not good at keeping my emotional distance, Matt.'

'I'm not going to fall for you and you're not going to fall for me, Stripes. We're both stronger than that.'

'You think?'

Matt dug deep for his most convincing tone. 'I know.'

'I'll hold you to those words, Cross. Okay, I'll sleep with you but don't blame me if this goes pear-shaped.'

'It won't. We won't let it.'

If that was what he believed, then why did those words feel like a lie? Why did he have a funny feeling in the pit of his stomach? And why couldn't he be smart and just leave Tori in the boxroom?

CHAPTER NINE

DAYS PASSED, sliding their way down to the festive season, and Tori found herself smiling through the days and laughing and loving through the nights. It was brilliant to have a man in her life who called when he said he'd call, who didn't break dates, who treated her with respect. She felt content, happy, secure and, best of all, she liked who *she* was with Matt. She was authentic Tori and she wasn't ever letting her go again. Being free to be herself was an empowering and liberating experience and she kept promising herself that she wouldn't put up with anything less if—when! when! when!—she and Matt parted ways.

Because they would part ways; that was the agreement. He would head south and she would be alone again. And, strangely enough, she was sort of okay with that. Oh, not with Matt going—how could she be?—but with the not-being-part-of-a-couple thing. She was starting to wrap her head around the concept of being alone, man wise, until someone decent came along again. He wouldn't be another Matt but maybe he would be a nice man. The word nice when it came to men was highly under-used, Tori decided. When you'd only had the not-so-nice, crazy and cockroachy type of men in your life, then you realised the value of nice.

And she was trying to be nice, well, nicer, as well. Matt had been away for a couple of days in Scotland dealing with his coke-addicted client—the man still wouldn't tell her who!—and was due home tonight so she thought that she'd prepare him a home-made meal, complete with candles and a pretty table. Of course, home-made meant lasagne made by Marco's mamma, so she was only fudging the truth a little. Alex and Lara were out, Poppy was on night shift and they had the house to themselves.

Maybe they could get creative in the kitchen...mmm.

'Hey, gorgeous.'

Tori spun around, dropped the handful of cutlery she was holding and screeched in fright at the big shadow in the doorway to the kitchen. When she opened her eyes again, Isaac had his shoulder pressed into the door frame and was laughing at her.

'Dammit, Isaac! You nearly made me wet myself.'

Isaac's dark eyes crinkled at the corners. 'Sorry, honey. This for me?'

'You wish.' Tori stepped forward to kiss his cheek, inhaled his spicy scent and sighed. Lord, the man was gorgeous and...Tori looked at him again...and nothing in her responded the way it normally did when a sexy, alpha-hot man walked into her life.

Normally she went into instant flirt mode and her body responded accordingly with either a tummy sparkle, a buzz in her head, hitched breath or prickly skin.

Matt Cross made her feel everything, all at once. Six times over.

Isaac was a good-looking guy, who should, under normal circumstances, be able to raise some sort of physical or mental response in her, just because he was standing there and breathing. But nothing.

'Matt Cross,' she muttered. It was all his fault. His, and his talented mouth and his wonderful hands and his crooked smile's, fault.

Damn. It.

Was he starting to spoil her for other men? What if he left and she never felt attraction to anyone ever again?

'Talking of...' Isaac said, snatching an olive from the bowl of salad on the table. 'Is he around?'

'He should be here soon. He's on his way in from Glasgow.' Tori gestured to the table. 'He's been away for a couple of days, hence the dinner.'

'You two have hooked up?'

'He didn't—?' *Tell you?* Tori finished the sentence in her head. Of course Matt hadn't—why would he? Isaac wouldn't tell Matt about the short-term, no-strings-attached relationships he had either. And why did that hurt? She pulled up her favourite don't-give-a-crap smile. 'Yeah, we've hooked up. Temporarily. No strings attached.'

'Okay.' Isaac sent her a doubtful look. 'May I point out that making him a nice welcome-home supper is not a NSA-type of thing to do?'

'No, you may not!' Tori snapped, her eyebrows pulling together. What should she do? Just shove a pizza at him and a napkin? Yeah, probably, sensible Tori spoke inside her head. Maybe the garlicky, meaty, fragrant pasta and the pretty plates and the open wine bottle and...and the flowers were a bit over the top?

A little? Maybe a lot OTT? She grabbed the wine bottle and dashed some into a glass and handed it to Isaac. 'Wine?'

Isaac took the glass with a lazy grin. 'Thanks. So, is Poppy around?'

'Night shift,' Tori replied, boosting herself up onto the counter. 'So, what is the deal between you and Poppy?'

An expression Tori couldn't identify, but one she thought might be a mixture of frustration, affection and dissatisfaction, passed over Isaac's face. 'There's nothing going on between Poppy and I...'

Tori cocked her head. 'Do you really expect me to believe that? Both of you act weird around each other and the tension factor redlines.'

'Not discussing it, Tori,' Isaac said, his tone genial but his eyes hard. Knowing that she was beaten, she changed the subject. 'So, how do you know Matt?'

'He hasn't said?'

No, that's why I'm asking you, she retorted, in her head. Matt doesn't talk about himself or his life or his friends. Actually, they rarely delved beneath surface stuff, Tori realised. Mostly because they were too busy getting their hands and mouths on each other. They'd known each other for a few weeks but she knew little about him and he even less about her.

They were not *confiders*, either of them.

Isaac pulled out a chair and dropped his long body into it. 'Alex and I attended the same boarding school until I was about fifteen…and I played cricket. Matt's school came over to the UK on a sports tour and we were both chosen to spend three weeks at a cricket academy during the school holidays. Matt and I became friends and stayed friends, even after I left that public school. When I was about seventeen, his dad paid for me to go over to South Africa to spend their summer holidays with them. Best Christmas I've ever had,' Isaac said wistfully.

'Sun, sand, girls and Matt's mum providing food on tap for you,' Tori joked.

Isaac sent her a strange look. 'Matt's mum died when he was young, Tori. He hasn't told you about his mum?'

Obviously not. Tori just shook her head.

Isaac looked momentarily uncomfortable. From his look Tori realised that there were no-strings-attached relationships and then there were 'NO STRINGS ATTACHED' relationships. She and Matt were obviously having the latter.

'It was Matt's dad, who I'm still crazy about, who fed and carted us from beach to beach and party to party. He's a great man.' Tori forced herself to concentrate on Isaac's words. 'You'd like him. And, I suspect, he'd like you.'

It didn't matter since she'd never get to meet him. Tori lifted her head as the front door opened and banged closed. Isaac cocked his head as they heard Matt's masculine rumble and an indistinguishable feminine reply. 'Matt's back... and Poppy. I thought you said she was on night shift,' Isaac said, and that funny look passed through his eyes again. Yeah, there was *nothing* going on between him and Poppy, her size-ten butt.

'She must have run home during her break. She sometimes does that.' Tori jumped off the counter and nudged his shoulder with her hip. 'Time for you to act weird and the tension to shoot up,' she teased.

'Brat.' Isaac slid his arm around her waist and dug his fingers into her ribs. Tori yelped, jumped and tumbled down into his lap, laughing as her bottom hit his knees and she bounced into his chest.

And that was how Matt and Poppy found them when they stepped into the kitchen five seconds later.

He'd failed, Matt thought, shoving his key into the lock at the flat in Lancaster Road. He'd failed at talking his client into rehab, failed to get through to him. He'd used every weapon in his arsenal—shouting, persuading, rationalising—but Jonas had just brushed him off, certain that he could handle his addiction and his career. When he finally got the message through that he had to choose between his career and coke, he'd chosen coke.

God. He still wanted to punch a wall, he was that angry, that disappointed. With Jonas and with himself.

'Hey, Matt.'

Matt turned and saw Poppy behind him and gestured her to walk into the hall in front of him. 'Tough day?'

'A bitch of a couple of days,' Matt admitted. He saw Poppy's scrubs below her coat. 'You working tonight?'

'Mmm, it's quiet so I thought I'd grab a bite to eat quickly.' Poppy sniffed. 'That smells like lasagne, yum.'

Matt followed Poppy through to the kitchen and stopped in the doorway. This was all he needed, he thought, taking in the scene in front of him. He was tired, wired and the last couple of days he'd felt as if life were scouring his soul with a Brillo pad. In normal circumstances he wouldn't be too worried about finding Tori in Isaac's lap—he trusted Isaac with his life and knew that their bro' code wouldn't allow him to make a move on his girl...

If Isaac knew that Tori was his, and Matt didn't think that he did. Isaac might have heard that she and the Dipstick had broken up but not that she'd moved on to him. Matt glared at Isaac's big hands—one rested lightly on her thigh and the other on her back—and Isaac must have seen something in his face because he instantly lifted them both.

Better...not great—great would be Tori climbing off his lap. But even more unsettling than Tori's arm around Isaac's neck was the scene behind them. A romantic table, candles, flowers, something that smelled delicious in the oven...

'You want to climb off Isaac, Stripes? Before I deck him?'

Not that he would, but it was a nice thought.

He ignored the look of surprise Isaac sent him. 'You've given her a nickname...*already*? You only ever do that to people who are—'

Matt pinned Isaac to his chair with a hard look. 'Shut the hell up, I. *Now.*'

He looked at Tori as she scooted off Isaac's lap and came towards him. Bare feet, a pretty dress, artfully pinned hair that would fall apart if he shoved his hands into it. Every cell in his body clanged a warning.

A scene set for romance, seduction…

Matt heard Isaac and Poppy's stilted conversation in the background as Tori approached him, looking to place a kiss on his mouth. At the last moment he moved his head so that her kiss fell on his jaw and then he felt even more of a fool. What was wrong with him? Tori bit her lip as she stepped back, confused and hurt. He fought against the urge to haul that slim body up against his and lose himself in her. He'd had a craptastic time in Glasgow, felt as if he'd been put through the wringer, but with Tori around he felt as if the world made sense again.

Your mom would hug me and all my broken pieces would stick back together.

Matt stepped away from Tori, his father's voice echoing in his head. Ignoring her puzzled face, he scrubbed his hand over his face, finally understanding exactly what he meant. And frustration and anger started in his stomach and worked their way up his gullet. He didn't want to feel like this, didn't want anything from this not so flaky woman except a good time, sex, some laughs. And finding her in his best friend's arms shouldn't make him want to punch something, coming home to her shouldn't make sense.

'I thought we'd have supper, catch up on what we've been up to,' Tori said in that bright voice she used when she wasn't feeling sure of herself. 'You're welcome to stay, Isaac. You too, Poppy.'

'Thank you, Martha Stewart,' he replied in a hot voice, 'but I ate on the plane.'

That was a lie and he ignored his stomach's protest that he was starving. It would have to suck it up; he was not going to sit down and pretend to play happy families. He'd had a happy family, had a freaking perfect family before cancer had sucked his mum's health, her spirit and then her *life*. He'd had happy and perfect, security and love in his two parents and then half of that died.

Whoah, whoa, whoah...stomp on the brakes! Where the hell did that come from and why was he connecting Tori cooking supper for him with the death of his mum? Why did her doing this scare the pants off him?

'Oh, nonsense, I know what you look like when you're hungry and you're starving!' Tori replied in an I-can-rescue-this-night voice. She dashed some wine into a glass and pushed it across the table in his direction. 'Have some wine and lighten up. Then we'll eat and you can tell me how Glasgow was.'

'I'm not talking about Glasgow or my clients so don't nag me about them.' Matt slapped his arms across his chest.

'What the hell is wrong with you, Cross? It was a simple comment—you don't need to take my head off,' Tori snapped. 'If you don't want to talk, then just say so. *Jeez.*'

He wished he could talk to her but how could he tell her that he'd failed, that a kid he cared about was sliding further into chronic addiction and there wasn't a damn thing he could do about it?

'I'll grab some lasagne to go if I can, Toz,' Poppy told Tori, sending him a hard glare. He'd forgotten that Poppy was there; frankly he didn't care. He just wanted to go up to his room, take a hot shower and pass out on his bed...

He most especially didn't want to think...to feel like this.

He didn't want to feel like someone who was feeling confused, unsettled, feeling more than he should. He never felt more than vague affection and it was bizarre that he was having these weird feelings for Tori, who refused to fit into any box. Beyond bizarre...maybe he was more tired than he thought.

Tori turned away to rummage in a cupboard for a container but not before he caught the hurt on her face, the glisten of tears in her eyes. Dammit. He looked at Isaac, who raised his eyebrows, and Matt didn't need more than two brain cells to interpret his look. Asshat about covered it.

He couldn't disagree.

'I wasn't expecting you back yet.' He grabbed Isaac's outstretched hand and bent over when Isaac pulled him towards him in a chest bump. Matt stayed there and spoke in a low tone only Isaac could hear. 'Nice to see you even if you did have your hands on my girl's ass.'

'And a very nice ass it is too. And you're acting like a two-year-old, Cross,' Isaac muttered back.

Matt reared back and glared at Isaac, who raised his hands. 'Hey, I call it like I see it.' He lifted his voice. 'And relax, I'm not back for good. I needed to check up on a couple of things with my business and popped by to see…you all,' Isaac replied, curiosity in those dark eyes. He flashed Matt a grin that usually meant he was about to stir the pot. 'Let me know when you're finished with the PMS and we'll catch up. Or I can just hand you your ass in the ring.'

PMS? Ouch.

Talking of, he could do with a workout session to get rid of his tension, some of this anger. Isaac stood up, shook his head, reading his mind. 'Not tonight, bro'.' He dropped his voice and Matt leaned forward to catch his words. 'If you weren't being such a chop you could've worked off that stress between the sheets. Moron.'

Isaac quickly walked over and placed a lingering kiss on Tori's cheek, which had Matt wanting to thump him again.

'Give him hell, gorgeous.' Isaac stepped up to Poppy and Matt watched Isaac grimace when Poppy stepped back to avoid his kiss. What was the deal with those two? He felt Isaac's fist clamp his shoulder and then he was walking out of the kitchen, Poppy, clutching her takeaway lasagne, following him out.

Tori switched off the oven, shoved the salad in the fridge and when she met his eyes again, hers were a deep blue and sparking with annoyance. 'Welcome home, Matt,' she said, her voice saturated with sarcasm. 'There's a hotwater bottle and aspirin in case you start with cramps too.'

Tori sat on the narrow bed in the boxroom, pillows under her butt and behind her neck, her laptop on her lap. She opened up her social media page and skimmed through the status updates from family and friends. Her father had recently been in New York and, judging by the photo of the blonde on his arm, was there with his latest gold-digger mistress bimbo. Her mother was in Vegas with her best friend, Janine. She'd won ten thousand dollars playing blackjack. Tori knew that she'd lose it on craps or the roulette table—money slid through her mum's fingers like baby oil.

Situation normal, then. Lucky them.

Tori tipped her head back so that it rested against the cold wall, listening to the water pipes creak and groan. Matt was in the shower…and instead of being in there with him, she was hiding out in her coffin, wondering when she'd become the village idiot.

She wasn't going to fall for him, she'd told herself. She wasn't going to place herself in the same position she'd found herself in so many times before, where she made all the effort and was given nothing in return. So why had she prepared that welcome-home meal? Why had she made the effort to do something nice for him? He'd sounded so drained, so weary when she'd spoken to him early that afternoon and she knew that something had gone wrong with his client in Glasgow, that the person in question was giving Matt grief. She'd heard it in his voice, heard the frustration and weariness.

He was fully invested in his clients and she, better than most, understood how draining the demands people made on your emotions could be. Hadn't she only ever hooked up with men who drained her of her energy? She'd fed their egos, reassured them, pandered to their needs. While it wasn't quite the same thing, Matt had a couple of clients who were, like her exes, difficult. Demanding. Spoilt.

He needed to give them boundaries, to explain that, while he was their manager, they weren't entitled to a regular pound of his flesh. He needed to protect himself, to guard against them sucking him dry...

God, she felt protective over him. Protective? Over that cool, calm, laid-back slab of muscle? When? How? And, dear God, why?

Tori banged her head against the wall. Matt didn't need her protection, her affection and, apparently, cosy sit-down dinners. He'd spelled it out, explained the rules and, as per normal, she was ignoring them, making up her own rules as she went along. What was wrong with her? He didn't want her for anything longer than a short-term fling, for some fun sex, a couple of laughs.

This wasn't going anywhere and she was done pretending that it was. Why did she always take so long to cotton on? Sex, laughs, short term, that was what he had offered. She always did this and she was falling into her bad habits again. Most of her boyfriends had started off as being a casual hook-up but she always, through charm and persistence, ended up forcing those men into becoming her boyfriends. How she did it she wasn't sure, but was it any wonder that none of those squished-into-a-relationship men worked out?

She was not going to repeat her past mistakes, she thought. And that meant no prying into his life, no getting-to-know-you conversations, no cosy dinners and no demands. And no believing in fairy tales and what ifs and manipulating him into a relationship...not that Matt could be manipulated, but the principle was what was important here.

This wasn't about love or a relationship or anything more than two bodies indulging in some mutual getting-your-rocks-off bedroom-based fun.

'Tori...'

Tori jerked her head up and looked at Matt standing in the narrow doorway, dressed in straight-legged sweat pants and a white tee. He was holding the door frame above his head and his biceps bulged against the fabric around his arms. His hair was wet and he looked exhausted. He had his ever-present mobile in his hand.

'So, how deep a hole am I in?' he asked, weariness in his eyes and tone of voice.

'Sorry?' Tori frowned. What was he talking about?

'You went to the effort to make me a nice meal and I spoilt it all by acting like a child. So, depth of hole and an indication of how much I should grovel would be helpful.'

'You're apologising?'

'Badly, apparently.' Matt dropped his arms, stepped into the coffin and sat on the end of her bed, lifting her feet to lay them across his thighs. He rested his head against the wall and sighed. 'Crappy, crappy couple of days and you didn't deserve me acting like a jerk.'

Uh... 'I thought you were cross with *me*. For overstepping the no-strings-attached line.'

Matt frowned as he rested his hand on her foot and tingles skittered up her legs and thighs. 'More with myself than you.'

'Care to explain that?' Tori asked.

Matt shook his head and Tori twisted her lips. Of course he wouldn't—they didn't go deep, she reminded herself.

'My client booked himself out of rehab, scored some coke and nearly OD'ed,' Matt said in a flat voice.

Uh…so much for not talking, Tori thought, scrambling to catch up. Then his damned mobile rang and, before he could answer it, Tori grabbed it and switched it off.

Seeing the protest on his lips, she shook her head. 'No, not tonight. They can all get along without you for one night.' She placed the phone under her butt and looked at him. 'Talk to me, Matt.'

'I went up there to try and persuade him to go back into rehab after he was released from hospital but he's not interested.' Matt scrubbed his face with his hands and cursed. 'Twenty-two years old, one of the most talented footballers in the sport and he's shoving his entire future up his nose. I could just…just…*belt* him!'

Tori pulled her feet back and scrambled up, instinctively climbing into his lap to give him any comfort she could.

'He doesn't know how lucky he is! I would've done anything to have his talent at sport, talent he's squandering! He's phenomenally good and this little stunt of his is going to cost him big. I warned him. I warned him so many times.'

Tori tucked her face into his neck as his arms came around her, pulling her closer. 'I'm sure you did all you could, Matt.'

'I can't get through to him, Tori. I can't make him see the consequences of his actions.'

'That's his choice, Matt. Not yours.'

Matt's voice was streaked with pained frustration. 'I keep thinking that I've failed him, that there was something more I could've done.'

'Honey, you're not the only person in his life. I presume he has coaches and family and team management who have tried to intervene.'

'Yes, but—'

'No buts, Matt. You've tried, they've tried. His choice, his consequences. You can't save everybody and you're not responsible for him.'

Matt was quiet for a long time. 'I'm going to have to dissolve his contract, to stop representing him.'

'Maybe that will be his wake-up call. But whatever happens you can walk away knowing that you did your best to help him—you can be utterly guilt free. There is nothing more you can do for him, Matt.'

Matt let out a deep, shuddery breath and rested his chin on top of Tori's head. He remained quiet for a long, long time and Tori knew that she just needed to stay where she was, in his arms, giving him silent support and comfort.

Right now, she was just being his friend; he didn't need her for anything more than to talk this through, for a little support of his own. She was not going to read anything more into being here, with him, than that.

She was done with imagining things that just weren't there.

CHAPTER TEN

MATT AND ALEX walked up the stairs to the flat, muscles protesting from spending Saturday morning in the gym. Alex had been thrilled at his invitation to join him in the boxing ring and he had been a worthy opponent. Fast, sneaky and, like Isaac, he had a hard right hook. Matt wiggled his jaw and frowned at the grin Alex sent him.

'God, it was so great to share some testosterone while I exercised. Nice change to put someone other than the lipstick-and-Lycra yummy-mummies through their paces, exercise-wise.'

Matt narrowed his eyes. 'You were putting me through the paces? I don't think so.'

Alex snorted. 'Please, you were winded at the end of five rounds.'

'So were you. And who whined when I tapped your nose?'

Alex gingerly touched his nose with the tips of his fingers. 'Damn, that hurt. Lucky it's not broken.'

'I pulled my punch,' Matt smugly told him, and grinned at Alex's glare. 'So, since you turned down my tickets to watch the game, what are your plans for this frigid Saturday?'

Alex shoved his key into the door of the flat and pushed it open. 'Yeah, I'm seriously bummed about that but I need to do some business stuff…get that out of the way so that it's not hanging over my head while we're in the Bahamas.' He flashed a satisfied grin. 'Sun and sex. Can't wait.'

'Lucky git,' Matt growled.

'Hey, you're heading back into the sun soon. Isaac said that he wanted to be back in the flat at the end of the month, which means you've got less than a week in the flat as well.'

And didn't that make him feel like throwing up all over his trainers? Professionally he could leave tomorrow; he'd done what he needed to do. He'd hired his London-based sports agent, an older guy with tons of contacts and experience, and he knew John was enormously capable and could find new premises for the UK office himself. He was only cooling his heels in London because of a certain gorgeous girl with eyes the colour of midnight.

Those strings were getting longer and stickier...

'Earth to Matt.' Alex waving a hand in front of his face jerked him back to the conversation.

'Uh...' Matt fumbled '...leaving...yeah...I have a couple more things to sort out but I should be done by the end of the month.'

'If you're not you're welcome to move into our room if you need more—' Alex glanced up the stairs '—time in London. So, are you still going to the game?'

Matt shrugged. 'Might as well. Tori's parents are both in London and they are getting together for lunch so I'm on my own for the day.'

'They asked her to lunch?' Alex snorted loudly and Matt lifted his eyebrows.

'I'll believe it when I see it,' Alex muttered as he threw his coat over the newel post of the stairs.

Matt, not having brother status, hung his jacket up on the hook and dropped his gym bag to the floor. 'Not reliable, then?'

'Oh, they'll be there unless something better comes up. Tori falls way, way down on their list of priorities.'

Matt shook his head, unable to comprehend that. He knew that he came first, second and third with his own dad and he knew, intrinsically, that it would've been the same situation with his mum. He intended to be exactly the same sort of dad with his kids—his kids would never doubt how much they were loved, treasured.

Kids? He pulled up short. Kids? When had he started thinking that kids were going to be part of his future, as natural an occurrence as breathing? Kids with his black hair and Tori's striking blue eyes...

Matt grabbed the newel post as his balance wavered and spots appeared behind his eyes. No, that couldn't be right. Tori was a short-term fling, a way to pass the time.

'You okay, mate?' Alex asked, frowning.

'Fine,' Matt ground out. And he would be as soon as he rid himself of the image of Tori rounded and luscious, carrying his child. Of Tori with a black-haired imp on her hip... God, he was losing it. Maybe Alex's right hook had dislodged something when it connected with his head earlier.

Like his entire freaking brain!

He needed a shower, to get a grip and to book himself a damned frontal lobotomy or a brain transplant.

Probably both.

After his shower Matt dressed in a pair of dark jeans and a long sleeved T-shirt, walked past the boxroom on the way to the kitchen and heard a faint noise coming from the room behind the partially open door. Reminded of last week's conversation with Poppy about the possibility of there being a resident rodent colony sharing the flat with them, Matt thought that he'd investigate the possibility.

Mice didn't scare him—back home they had bigger and

meaner wildlife that occasionally invaded their homes. Matt nudged open the door to the room with his foot and jerked his head when he saw Tori on the end of the bed, her face carefully blank. She was dressed in a white turtle-neck, scarlet tailored shorts over black tights. Short black boots with a spiked heel completed the sexy outfit.

'Tori? What's going on? I thought you were going to lunch with your parents,' Matt said, reaching over her to switch on the butt-ugly lamp that provided the only light in the room.

'Yeah, so did I,' Tori said, her tone and voice robotic. She waved at her mobile, which lay on the bed next to her. 'They cancelled.'

'Both of them?' Matt questioned.

Tori dredged up a smile but Matt discerned the hurt under the layer of embarrassment in her eyes.

'This happen often?' he asked, sitting on the bed next to her.

Tori pulled her bottom lip between her teeth. 'All my life. Guess I'm the fool for believing that things might change. Anyway, it really doesn't matter.' She jumped up and started to fold up the clothes she'd slung over the clothes rail. The fact that she was trying to fold a bulky coat was a huge hint that her insouciance was an act.

'It does matter, Victoria. It matters a lot. They are idiots not to want to spend time with you,' he said, his voice radiating conviction. Mostly because he believed every word he was saying.

Tori stared at the lamp, rapidly blinking her eyes. When a tear rolled out she angrily, hastily, wiped it away. 'Don't, Matt.'

'Don't what?'

'Don't be nice to me.'

Matt cocked his head. 'Why not?'

Two more tears rolled. 'Because I'm not used to guys

being nice to me… God, I don't think my ex…exes even knew I had parents.' Tori wiped her tears away with her fingertips. 'And when you're nice to me I end up crying…'

'Well, don't—I can't handle your piggy-on-crack face.' Matt scrunched up his eyes and grinned when he heard Tori's wobbly chuckle. God, he could listen to her laugh for the rest of his life…

For the rest of his life. His breath caught in his throat. What. The. Hell?

For the rest of his life? That was a long time… For the next week, a couple more months, a couple more years but *the rest of his life*? Alex's punch to his head must've caused more damage than he'd realised.

'Why are you looking at me like that?' Tori asked.

Matt, eventually, found the words. 'Like what?'

'Like I'm a three-headed alien.' Tori tipped her head and gestured with her hands. 'You're looking at me like you're actually seeing me for the first time.'

Because he was—not as a quick fling or a way to pass time but as a woman: fragile but incredibly strong, vulnerable but brave, sexier than he ever imagined. He was looking at her like that because his world suddenly made sense. So, okay, she wasn't who he'd expected to one day want to settle down with, she was uptight and sometimes high maintenance, essentially lonely but fiercely loyal. She was everything he'd never thought he needed but so did…

For the first time in his life the fear of not being with her nearly outstripped the fear of loving and losing someone.

Nearly but not quite…

Instead of throwing his heart on the floor at his feet as a part of him wanted to do, Matt offered her another suggestion. 'Hey, Drew gave me tickets to watch his team play this afternoon. Want to come with me?'

'Who? What?'

'Rugby, Stripes.' He rolled his eyes. 'Jeez.'

Tori tipped her head. 'By the way, what did Isaac mean when he made that comment about you giving me a nickname? He didn't finish his sentence...something like you only give nicknames to people who are...what?'

Matt stared down at his feet and cursed the heat he felt on his cheeks. 'Uh...um...it's just a mark of affection, acceptance. Fondness.'

He didn't tell her that, in the Cross household, nicknames were for people who'd been in their lives a long time, for people who would always be in their lives. Important people.

'So, about that rugby?' he asked, desperate to change the subject.

Tori wrinkled her nose. 'It's cold out there and rugby... really? I'm not a rugby type of girl.'

'Well, I'm very much a rugby type of guy so humour me.' Matt looked at her long legs in those opaque tights and nodded at her feet. 'Though you might want to swap those silly boots for something practical and put some jeans on over those tights.'

'Only if you buy me a bang-up lunch first,' Tori demanded.

'Sure,' Matt agreed. 'Fish and chips and mushy peas?'

Tori swore that the earth shook when a seven-foot-tall and six-foot-wide rugby player literally ran over a much smaller player from the opposing team. Ouch! Watching from the box seats directly over the centre line, Tori whimpered in sympathy as the downed player lay on his back on the freezing pitch.

'Wuss,' Matt stated and Tori shook her head. This was a game for Neanderthals, she thought as the injured player was hauled to his feet and limped back to join the game.

Tori dropped lower into her seat, ignoring Matt's shouts, yells and groans, and thought back to their conversation in the flat, the strange look on Matt's face after her silly comment about him seeing her for the first time. If she were still the old Tori, she would be spinning stories in her head, dreaming big dreams and reading far too much into his expression. She'd be off on a tangent by now, picking out white dresses and bridesmaids and naming their children.

The old Tori could make a mountain out of a grain of sand and she wouldn't do it this time; she refused to. That look on Matt's face was not tenderness and affection or any of love's many cousins. And what she and Matt had was nothing more than a fling: a fling that was due to end in about a week or so. It had to end in a week or so because by then Matt would be room-less and bed-less and, as much as she craved his body, it was physically impossible, and possibly dangerous, to attempt to make love on Izzy's childhood bed.

Of course, since Alex and Lara's room would be empty... No, dammit, she was not going there! This...*thing*...was ending and she was okay with it.

She'd spent many, many, many hours in mental preparation for it to be over and she was not going to let all that effort go to waste. She was the new and improved Tori and she would say goodbye to Matt with dignity and self-respect.

She would not throw herself at his feet and demand that he love her.

Tori jumped as Matt flew out of his chair and pumped his arm in the air. Something major must have happened but she shrugged it off as Matt dropped into an excited conversation with the equally rugby-mad man on his right... excellent try, fancy footwork, blah, blah.

She had to say goodbye to Matt, just to prove that she could. She wanted to show to herself that she could be on her own, that she was strong enough, confident enough to navigate her life by her own compass.

She was her own North Star and she would never, ever beg a man to love her again.

Besides, all this introspection was a waste of time; she was reading far too much into the look on Matt's face anyway. It meant nothing, could mean nothing.

Feeling emotionally steadier, she looked at Matt's profile, his face wreathed in enjoyment. It was starting to get dark, she thought, looking up at the sky. The stadium lights were illuminating the field.

The noise of the crowd dulled to a roar as Matt turned to look at her, his eyes sparkling with pleasure. 'Helluva try, Stripes.'

'Helluva try,' Tori said, mostly because she had no idea what else to say. Matt's mouth tipped up at the corners as he wrapped his arm around her shoulder and pressed his admittedly freezing but very fine lips into her temple.

'You're a sport, Toz.'

'Glad to hear it. Listen, while you are thinking that I am wonderful, will you do me a favour?' Tori asked, biting the inside of her lip.

'If I can.'

'My company is having an awards evening and it would be nice if I had someone to go with me.' She didn't tell him that she was up for an award for the work she'd done on the charity function, but it would be so nice for once to have someone in the audience looking proud. 'It's a pretty big deal.'

'Sure. When?'

Tori gave him the date and watched as Matt plugged it into his mobile, his eyes flitting between the game and his mobile. 'Done.'

Tori closed her eyes in relief and the loud siren made them fly open again. She looked around and saw that players were running off the field. 'Yay, we're done! Let's get some grub.'

Matt laughed. 'Sorry, sweetheart, that's the whistle for half-time. We've still got forty minutes to go.'

They found a table inside a pub close to the stadium and Tori wrapped her hands around a cup of hot chocolate and hoped that she would start to defrost soon. Matt sipped at his glass of beer and their silence was comfortable, introspective, gentle.

'Pass me your phone,' Tori demanded.

Matt rolled his eyes but handed it over. Tori hit the power button and tucked it into her bag.

'I take it that I am off duty for a while?'

'Yep.' Tori smiled at him. 'Do you have a problem with that?'

'Not at all. Thanks for coming with me. I had fun,' Matt commented. 'And sorry that you were bored to tears.'

'It wasn't so bad,' Tori replied with a small smile. 'Watching all those fit, gorgeous men get sweaty is never a complete waste of time.'

Matt laughed. 'Glad you could find something about it that you liked. Not into sports, then?'

'I suck at everything, including running. Ask Poppy and Izzy. They occasionally make me but I bitch and moan or talk so much that we rarely get anywhere.' Tori perked up. 'But I do skate. There's a Winter Wonderland festival happening at Hyde Park—we should go skating. Do you skate?'

'Uh…no.'

Tori placed her hand on her heart and faked astonishment. 'A sport Matt Cross hasn't mastered? Be still my beating heart.'

'I live in Africa. No snow, little ice,' Matt pointed out. 'And who wants to be inside a rink when the sun is shining? Where did you skate?'

'There's a shallow pond behind Ridley Hall and it al-

ways freezes in winter. My grandfather taught us to skate,'
Tori mused.

'Parents too busy?' Matt asked.

'Too uninterested,' Tori admitted. 'My parents have
a very nebulous concept of commitment, fidelity or integrity.'

'Why on earth did they get married in the first place?'
Matt leaned forward, his eyes on her face.

Tori smiled as a little girl, maybe not quite four, walked
around the table opposite to where they were sitting and
climbed up and into her father's lap and instantly fell
asleep. Such trust, such love...

'I've thought about that quite often and I think it's because they recognised each other.'

Tori crossed her legs, blew on the steaming liquid in
her cup and took a sip before speaking again. 'I think that
they instinctively saw the flip side of their coin—they are
both equally good-looking, equally selfish, equally narcissistic, came from equally moneyed families. They were,
are, a good fit. They can't hurt each other.'

'But they can hurt you.'

Tori winced at his perceptiveness. 'My mum once told
me that she never meant to have children, that I was a result of her forgetting to take the pill because she was drunk
for most of the first year of her marriage.'

'Nice.' Matt ground out the word.

'God, they are so damn embarrassing. I have a theory
about how I'm going to raise my kids, if I ever get to have
any,' Tori said, her eyes sparkling. 'Want to hear it?'

'You want kids?'

'I really do. One day. So, about that theory...'

'Go for it.'

'It's very complicated and high falutin',' Tori warned,
her smile flashing.

'Falute away.'

'I'm just going to do everything my folks didn't do, and the little they did do, I'm going to do the exact opposite,' Tori stated, a tad triumphantly.

Matt laughed. 'Complicated and high falutin' indeed. That sounds like an excellent plan, Stripes. I think you're going to be a brilliant mum.'

Tori nodded. 'Some day,' she softly said.

After a couple of minutes, Matt placed his glass on the table and folded his arms. He looked out of the window and watched as fat snowflakes drifted down. 'God, my mum would've loved this snow. She loved winter.'

'What's your favourite memory of her?' Tori asked, her heart bumping at the grief she still saw in his eyes, the hole in his soul that had never, would probably never, close.

Matt shot her a quick look. 'You know that she died?'

'When you were young. Isaac told me.'

Matt blew air into his cheeks. 'I should've told you, but talking about my mum is tough for me.'

'Yeah, I understand that. We both would rather pull our teeth out with pliers than talk about our feelings and, besides, we don't have the relationship that has allowed that sort of sharing.'

That same look from earlier flashed across Matt's face and he opened his mouth to say something and Tori instinctively realised that she wasn't ready to hear what he was about to say. She knew that his words would shift the dynamics of their no-strings relationship and she couldn't deal with it.

Not when she'd tried so hard, had come so far to keep herself detached.

Matt started to speak and Tori spoke right over him. 'So, about that childhood memory?'

Matt opened his mouth again, closed it and rubbed his jaw, his deep green eyes intense. She held her breath, waiting to see if he would push, and felt inordinately relieved when he answered her question. 'It's a Christmas memory, actually; she always wanted to experience a white Christmas. It would be thirty-five degrees outside but she always put fake snow on the windows, a plastic snowman on the front lawn. We made reindeer food, put glitter down on the grass in wide stripes so that they had a landing strip…'

Tori smiled, imagining a gap-toothed, six-year-old Matt running around on Christmas Eve, bubbling over with excitement. 'But what really amazed the hell out of me was the layer of snow in front of the tree and the size-nine boot prints in the snow.'

Oh…oh, what a cool idea. Tori filed that in her mental when-I-have-kids file and leaned forward, entranced by Matt's faraway voice.

'She must have got up extra early to scrape all that ice out of the freezer, but those boot prints in ice kept me believing in Father Christmas a lot longer than most of my mates.'

'God, she sounds amazing. Were the two of you close?'

She saw the apple in his throat bob, picked up the tightening of his hand around his glass. His eyes went bleak and faraway and she didn't need him to answer but he spoke anyway. 'Yeah…we were tight. She was so…into me, in the non-creepiest, best way possible. She'd tell me that she was my parent first and my friend second and that it was her job to ride my ass but living with her was…fun. Flat-out fun.'

'You still miss her.'

'I miss her every damn day. A piece of my heart died when she did. And a whole lot of my faith and trust in God and life.' Matt looked down and stared at his feet. 'And she and my dad, they were like…'

'Soul mates?'

'Yeah. That.' Matt jammed his hands into his hair.

'When she died, that first year afterwards, my dad… It was brutal.'

'It could only have been.'

'I used to listen to him weep, night after night. It killed me… I swore I would never, ever love someone that much, put myself in that position of having my heart ripped out like that.' Matt raised his head and his eyes, deep and mesmerising, slammed into hers. 'I promised myself.'

Tori felt her throat close, felt her heart pick up speed and her eyes widened. She held her breath, terrified that his next words would tip her off that pedestal she'd climbed up onto; the one that was safe, and tidy and not complicated at all.

Out of the corner of her eye Tori saw the waiter approaching their table and she flicked him a brief glance, her concentrated attention on Matt's mouth, waiting for him to finish that statement. In her head, want and dread duked it out to see which one would be the dominant emotion.

It turned out neither would have the pleasure because, instead of explaining, Matt took the menu the waiter held out and flipped it open. 'I'm starved—let's eat.'

Tori opened her mouth to protest and quickly shut it again. If he said anything else then she would have to respond, to accept that something was changing between them, and she wasn't ready to deal with change, to shift her thinking. It was better that they just carried on as they were before, drifting in a sexual haze.

Anything deeper had the power to make her dream and hadn't life shown her that, time and time again, her dreams had a way of blowing up in her face?

CHAPTER ELEVEN

THERE WAS SOMETHING about a little red dress, Tori decided, sliding her hands over her hips and twisting sideways to make sure that the low dip in the back fell on the right side of sexy.

Yep, that worked, she decided. Sexy but not trashy and Matt would love it. He would especially like the fact that one tug of the tie at the back of her neck would have the frothy dress falling to the floor and she would be naked except for the tiniest pair of lace panties, a garter belt, stockings and a sexy pair of stilettos.

Then again, Matt was fairly easy to please—she just had to get naked to put a smile on his face. The trick, she decided as she fiddled with her hair, was getting out of the flat without getting naked because if they did then they would be late and, as much as she adored making love with Matt, being late for the BB&K awards evening was not an option.

Tori glanced at the bedside clock, winced at the time and was considering going to haul Matt out of the shower when he stepped into the room, a towel tied around his hips, droplets of water still clinging to his hair, his broad chest.

He tossed her a glance and headed straight for his tux that he'd tossed onto his bed. Tori tapped her foot and waited and not two seconds later he straightened, turned around and let out a low, very appreciative whistle.

'Wow, Stripes. You look…'

Yep, his mouth dropped open as he lifted his hand, extended his index finger and drew a circle in the air. Tori obediently pirouetted. Matt took two strides, reached her and his hand went to the back of her neck and started to fiddle with the ties that held the halter neck up.

Tori slapped his hands away. 'Get off me, Cross! We're going to be late!'

'I'll be quick,' Matt assured her, his other hand slipping under the red fabric to hold her breast, his thumb flicking over her nipple. As always, Tori's nipple bloomed and swelled in his hand.

She jumped backwards and used both hands to bat him away. 'Get dressed, you lunatic!' She saw his mouth descending and slapped both hands on his bare chest. 'And don't you dare kiss me—you'll smudge my make-up!'

'I prefer the more natural look anyway.' Matt told her, placing both hands on her face and swooping his mouth across hers. His tongue dipped and dived; Tori felt herself, and her carefully applied lipstick, melting.

Dammit, Cross, she thought even as she linked her arms around his neck and pressed herself into his damp chest. Matt grabbed her butt and lifted her up and into him, his erection testing the white towel and pushing her red dress between her thighs.

'Matt, we can't—'

'We can…' Matt muttered, pushing her dress up and over her hips, groaning when he saw her tiny, barely there panties. 'God, you kill me. You are so utterly beautiful.'

Okay, maybe they had time for a quickie, Tori decided. She could repair her make-up in the taxi; she could… Tori felt cool air on her naked breasts and realised that he'd undone the ties holding her dress up and then Matt was pulling her nipple deep into his mouth and she felt heat and lust pool between her legs.

It still felt like the first time, Tori thought in bewildered wonder. Still so hot, so wild, so passionate. Touching him was still a pleasure she couldn't get enough of: strong muscles under warm, masculine skin; his broad shoulders, his hard ass. He was both a fantasy and a wondrous reality, tough but gentle, demanding but tender...

Matt pulled away and Tori frowned. It took her a moment to realise that his mobile was chirping. 'Ignore it,' she murmured against his mouth.

'I would but it's the fourth missed call in as many minutes. Someone wants to talk to me rather badly.' Matt tapped her bottom to get her to release him and Tori pouted as she dropped her arms and stepped away. She pulled up the straps to her dress and retied the knot behind her neck, glancing at the mirror.

Make-up more or less intact, mouth needed redoing. Hair still good. Matt just needed to listen to his messages and get dressed. They would still get to the venue in plenty of time.

'I just need to return this call. I'll be quick, I promise.'

Tori closed her eyes in dismay. Matt's calls, as she'd learned over the past couple of weeks were never quick, especially if he was talking to one of his clients. 'Can't you leave it until the morning—?'

'Hey, bud. I've got your message—you sound desperate.'

Tori was working up quite a head of steam when Matt snapped his mobile closed a minute later and headed for the dresser and yanked out a pair of jeans. 'I've got a problem, Tori.'

'No! No, no, no, no, no, no!' Tori pointed to the tuxedo trousers. 'Whatever it is, it can wait. I've got to get to the awards ceremony and you're coming with me!'

'I'm sorry but this is an emergency.' Matt grabbed a sky-blue shirt and a black cashmere sweater from another drawer.

'Matt, I need you tonight. Please…I'm begging you here.'

Matt sent her a regretful look. 'My footballer…the one who dropped out of rehab—'

'He's not even your client any more!' Tori protested. 'You said you dropped him.'

'He's in London, sitting at the bar at the hotel I normally stay at, trying not to call his dealer to score some coke. He needs me.' Matt yanked the jersey over his head. 'He's twenty-two and scared out his mind. He's trying to do the right thing and he called me. I can't just leave him there and swan off to a function I don't have to go to anyway!'

Of course he couldn't. Matt didn't know how important this was to her. She hadn't told him she was nominated for an award. If she did, would he stay? She opened her mouth to ask him and abruptly closed it again.

No, she couldn't ask him to do that, not with someone's life at stake. Matt was always going to have people who needed him. Would she ever come first? Maybe it wasn't possible for her to have a long-term relationship with Matt, she realised. She wasn't his number-one priority, in his current crisis she didn't expect to be, but she kept forgetting. And, despite the severity of the situation, she just couldn't help but feel a little disappointed…a lot disappointed. She knew it was silly—selfish, even—but she just couldn't help it.

Yet again, even all dressed up and looking sensational, she wasn't enough. She wasn't enough when she was four and had split her head open and was taken to hospital by her nanny, because her parents were out. At fourteen when they'd promised to take her to the ballet, gave her money for a dress and forgot to come home from the races to take her. At sixteen, seventeen, last week.

She, simply, wasn't enough.

Matt sat down on the edge of the bed and pulled on his socks. 'Look, depending what time I get back, I could meet you there.'

But then he would've missed the award ceremony, she would've missed seeing the pride on his face, his approval. That was why she wanted him there—just once, to have someone standing in her corner, cheering her on.

She stared down at her feet, still encased in her kick-butt shoes.

'No, this is more important. It doesn't matter. Really. I'll be fine.'

Would she be fine? She wasn't sure. Tori knew that she was sliding into a vortex of destructive thoughts, knew that if she didn't stop the train of awful, self-deprecating memories she'd slide back into that morass of insecurity and anguish she'd worked so damn hard to climb out of.

Tori stepped out of her shoes, bent down to pick them up and held them in her hands. Her bottom lip wobbled and she tugged it between her teeth and bit down, to keep both it, and her tears, under control. Matt looked at her before sliding on his flat leather boots. 'We okay, Tori?'

Tori managed to smile. 'Yeah. Sure. I need to get going or else I'll be late.'

Tori sat on the edge of her bed in the boxroom, the trophy awarded to her for the excellent work she'd done on the charity campaign last month in front of her. A part of her wanted to dismiss the pride she felt, the glow of success she felt in her stomach. Did the award mean anything if the people whose approval she needed most didn't know about it?

Did the tree falling in the forest still make a noise if there was no one around to hear it?

This award was proof that she was doing something right in her career but her personal life was still messy, uncertain... Had anything really changed since she'd walked out of Mark's flat?

Tori rested her elbows on her knees and stared at the awful shag carpet below her feet. What had actually changed? Nothing really. She was still in a relationship that wasn't going anywhere. Matt was going somewhere, back home...but they were going nowhere together.

And even if they tried to keep it going, the deck was stacked against them. Different continents, two careers, Matt's total commitment to his clients. His work and his people, clients and staff, would always come first with him and she needed more than that. She was worth more than that. And maybe, just maybe, that was okay.

I *need* more, Tori decided. I need more than a part-time man whose attention I'd have to fight for. I need more than good sex and laughs. I want commitment and hope and possibilities. Matt, with his drive to serve his clients and his issues around love and commitment, was not going to give that to her. Hadn't he perfectly demonstrated it earlier? One minute he was kissing the hell out of her and then his mobile rang, his switch flipped and he was gone—physically, mentally, emotionally. She felt... inconsequential. Unimportant. And, while she knew that he was just a temporary fling, she felt used. She no longer liked feeling used...

And this was how she'd carry on feeling if she allowed this fling to continue. She could fool herself and say that having half of something would be better than having nothing at all but, from the bottom of her soul, she knew that half of whatever Matt could give her would be a lot harder than having nothing.

She wanted someone who could love her without fear, without restrictions. It wasn't something she'd ever had probably because she believed that she never deserved it. Tori looked at the award again—maybe she did deserve it. Maybe, like the award she'd won tonight, she deserved it all.

She deserved more than this horrid room, and if her time had passed in this wonderful flat, then she should look for her own place, as soon as possible. She definitely deserved more attention from her useless parents but they were not going to change so she'd stop expecting it, stop setting herself up for disappointment.

And she deserved a man who would be her soft place to fall. She no longer needed someone to take care of her but someone to stand in her corner, cheering her on, would be nice. One day, hopefully sooner rather than later, she'd find the strength to let the memories of Matt drift away and she could start looking for someone else...

Because Matt hadn't promised her more than a fling, some fun, to be someone to teach her how she should be treated by a man. He'd done his job really well but it was time to let him go, time to say goodbye.

Because if she didn't do it now, tonight, she didn't know if she'd find the strength to do it again.

And this time, for the first time, she'd behave with dignity, self-respect, integrity.

In other words she'd act like an adult and not an impulsive girl.

When he returned to the flat too many hours later Tori was sitting on the stairs leading to the turret room, dressed in a pair of fuzzy sweatpants and her hair pulled back into a messy ponytail. Her face was clean of make-up and she held a half-drunk cup of cocoa in her hands.

She looked exhausted and...distant. His heart tumbled and sighed. What was he going to do about her?

He'd come so close, tonight, to blowing off his client to go with Tori to her function. If he had, there was no doubt that he'd be dealing with a strung-out, coked-up young man and the blame would rest squarely on his shoulders. It had been too close for comfort.

If that had happened how could he look at himself in the mirror?

Tori had a way of changing his priorities, his firmly held views on what he wanted for his life. She made him question whether he could live without love—a position he'd held firm for twenty-two years. She made him question his commitment to his clients, his career...and she split his focus. How could he give them a hundred per cent when she needed his attention too?

Yet she made him feel emotions he'd buried with his mother, she made him laugh and think and...feel but at what cost? And those emotions she pulled to the surface scared the hell out of him. Petrified was too tame a word for how they made him feel and the thought of dealing with them on an ongoing basis iced his blood.

Apart from those concerns, could he live with the consequences of the choices he made when he factored her into the equation?

He'd come so close to messing up tonight, to putting her first, and if he had the consequences could have been catastrophic.

Could he run that risk again? He didn't know...

'Hey,' he said, shrugging out of his leather jacket and running a hand through his hair for the umpteenth time that night. 'What are you still doing up?'

'Waiting for you.' Tori put her cup on the stair next to her and wrapped her arms around her knees. 'How's the kid?'

Matt shrugged as he dropped to sit on the step next to

her. 'He had bad withdrawal symptoms. I managed to get him into a clinic for this evening. They'll look after him tonight and he's agreed to go back to rehab in the morning.'

'Are you going to represent him again?' Tori asked.

Matt shrugged. 'I'll see. The most important thing is that he gets clean.'

Tori bit her lip and shifted away from him, closer to the wall. Matt frowned as she put some distance between them. 'I'm glad he's okay.' She stared at a spot between her feet. 'Can we talk?'

Matt closed his eyes. Here it comes, he thought. She was going to ask for more, ask for whatever this was between them to carry on, to go beyond the fling he'd promised her. What was he going to say? A part of him, a huge part of him, wanted to say yes but too much could go wrong... The emotional risk would be huge, to both of them.

He didn't think he could do it...

'I think we should call this quits,' Tori said in a quiet voice. 'I think it's time to say that we've had a fun time but it's over, that it's time to move on.'

'What?'

Had he heard her right? She was dumping him? *Them?*

Tori pulled her bottom lip beneath her teeth and held up her hand. 'I don't want to make this difficult, ugly. I've always had difficult and ugly when I've parted ways with men and I really want this to be different. I want to kiss your cheek and thank you for the best time of my life...for holding me and making love to me, for making me laugh and making me...better. I just want to say that.'

Matt ran an agitated hand over his face. 'I...didn't...I thought that you...'

'Wanted more?' Tori asked, tipping her head. She shrugged delicately and lifted a shoulder. 'I do want more but I know that I can't ask you to give me what you can't. Time, attention, commitment. So, when I get you out of my system—and that might take some time—I'm going to look for someone who can. Someone like you, who is a good man, an honest man. Someone who treats me well and who thinks that his sun rises and sets with me.'

'Tori...'

Tori stood up, all grace and dignity, and he thought that he'd never seen her so beautiful, so together, so poised... even though tears were running down her face. She bent down, placed her mouth on the corner of his and he inhaled her breath, her scent, her essence. 'Thank you, Matt. For everything. Have a wonderful life.'

For a long time after she left Matt just sat on the stairs, trying to wrap his head around what had just happened.

Prior to Matt leaving her life Tori would've said that she knew pain, that she was good friends with it. She hadn't had a cooking clue, she realised when she came home from work the next day to find the bedroom they'd shared stripped of Matt's belongings.

There were no clothes in the closets, the bedside table was clear of the sports magazines that had piled up there, his alarm clock, his e-reader. The silver-framed photograph of him and his dad was gone... Matt was gone.

Dear Lord, the reality of that statement sank in as Tori closed the door to the bedroom behind her. Matt. Was. Gone.

She had chased him away.

Pain, true pain, wasn't just a mild mixture of hurt and disappointment and regret as she'd always thought, but it had the depth of a dinosaur bite, the sting of molten lava. It was fire and acid and hell and...dear Lord, it hurt. Every cell of her body screamed in agony.

She'd done the right thing, she frantically told herself. She had. It would have hurt so much more—she couldn't imagine how but it would—if she'd allowed the situation to continue.

There were so many reasons why this couldn't work, she reassured herself as she paced the room where they had loved so often and so well. She sank to her haunches and wrapped her arms around her bent legs. She was demanding and melodramatic and he'd have to anchor her to earth. He came from a stable, loving family situation and she was the product of a dysfunctional train wreck of a marriage. She was insecure, he was confident. And he lived and worked a million miles away.

Tori felt panic, hot and wild, in her throat. This wasn't the way it was supposed to be, she thought, resting her cheek on her knees. She wasn't supposed to be feeling this empty, this wretched. He was supposed to be a fling, someone she could use and enjoy and walk away from without a backward glance. He was supposed to be the stepping stone to the new Tori, someone who could stand on her own two feet, who didn't need the approval of men to feel whole.

But as hard as she didn't want to, she had to accept that she'd done this far too many times, had been in this situation often enough to know the difference between love and infatuation; this time it was different—this time she was in love.

She was in love…utterly, hopelessly. For the first time. Properly.

He'd been caught off guard by her declaration to end it last night; she'd seen the confusion in his eyes, the regret, uncertainty. But she knew that he would get over her soon, would maybe even feel mild regret for the temperamental girl he once knew but his heart would soon recover.

But she doubted if hers ever would.

Matt pushed his sweat-soaked hair off his forehead with the back of his wrist and silently cursed when his kick-boxing sparring partner lifted his gloved hands in defeat, blood trickling from his nose. Damn, he hadn't thought he'd ploughed his fist into his face hard enough to make the guy bleed.

He felt bad about that. He had no right to be in the boxing ring, taking out his frustration on anyone stupid enough to take him on. But wailing on a punch bag didn't require the same levels of concentration dodging human fists and feet did. The bag also didn't allow him to be, momentarily, distracted from thinking of Tori, from his aching heart.

It was a sad state of affairs that he preferred to get punched in the head or kicked in the ribs than think about a woman.

'Matthew, that's enough.'

Matt heard the order in his father's voice and flicked him a glance. He was standing on the floor below the ring, his brow creased in worry.

'Enough now. Take a shower and then we're going to talk.'

'Not today, Dad.' Matt pulled at the ties on his gloves with his teeth.

'Matthew.' Patrick waited until Matt met his eyes and when he did, he spoke again. 'That wasn't a suggestion. Take a shower and meet me at the coffee shop on the corner. Do not make me chase down your ass.'

Matt cursed and knew that there was no way he could avoid a conversation with his dad, not when he had his stubborn face on. Ducking through the ropes, he grabbed his towel from a bench and draped it over his bare shoulder and headed towards the showers. He hadn't been back in Cape Town for long, yet every day was an exercise in resisting the temptation to get his butt back on a plane so that he could throw himself at her feet.

And say what?

He just had to endure these endlessly long days and then, hopefully some time soon, he would stop missing her, stop thinking about her.

Matt rested his forehead on the white tiled wall as steaming water pounded down his back. Heartache... he'd heard of the concept but he'd never thought that he would be experiencing it himself. In between the flashes of pain, he felt anaesthetised and detached, constantly aware that something appalling had just blindsided him. How—why—had he let this happen? He'd always been so careful not to put himself in this position of being emotionally hijacked by another person yet here he was, coming undone.

He simply couldn't work out how it had all come to pass. Sex, women and his interactions with them had always been a fun, adrenaline filled pastime, something he could pick up and discard at whim. Getting to know a new woman, her likes and dislikes in the bedroom, had always been fun but invariably, and quite quickly, began to wane. That hadn't happened with Tori...

Maybe because you haven't known her for that long. Given time it might still come to pass.

Except that it wouldn't because there was something fundamentally different about sex with Tori and it was simple: it wasn't sex, it was making love—a term he'd always scoffed at before. He had, in an obscenely short space of time, become attached—bonded, emotionally connected—to the crazy person.

God help him.

Because he had no idea about what to do or how to do it and he simply couldn't conceive of a life without her in it.

CHAPTER TWELVE

'YOU LOOK LIKE something the dog dragged in,' Patrick told him when he dragged a chair out and plonked himself down across the table from him in the crowded coffee shop.

'Thanks.' Matt scowled at him and looked out of the window to the blue sky, the six-foot waves rolling in on the beach beyond the promenade. It was a perfect summer's day and he wanted grey and drizzly, mucky weather. He didn't want to be here in the sunshine if Tori was in the wet and cold.

'Talk to me, Matt.'

Matt lifted his shoulder, still staring at the blue green sea. 'Surf's up.'

Patrick leant across the table and tapped the back of Matt's head with his hand. 'Talk. To. Me.'

Matt rubbed the back of his head, scowled again and ordered an espresso from the hovering waitress. When she was gone, he blew out a long breath and twisted his lips. 'You know that fling I was having?'

'With the PR girl? Tori?'

'Yeah. Not so much of a fling as I wanted it to be.' Matt glared at his parent. 'And I swear if you laugh, I'm getting up and walking away.'

Patrick made an effort at holding in his smile. 'You've got feelings for her?'

'Feelings? That's one way of putting it.' Matt tipped his

head back and looked at the ceiling. This was the perfect time, the perfect opening to finally verbalise the crazy thoughts of the last week or so. Except that he could think of a million things he'd rather be doing than expressing his wobbly, brand-new feelings.

'She's mine.' Then the words fell out of him, tripping over themselves to be heard. 'Even when she's overreacting, is tense or stressed or acting slightly crazy, she's still endearing because I *get* her. I understand the source of her insecurity, understand her need for assurance. When you are never anyone's priority, when you never come first, disappointment and disillusionment come quickly and emotional fortitude and the ability to roll with the punches isn't developed.' That night of the awards, he should've remembered that, should've taken the time to explain his actions better, to reassure her.

Matt ran a hand through his hair. Tori…everything he'd never thought he'd want but the sum total of what he needed. 'She makes me laugh and she makes me think. I feel protective over her… She's my lightning bolt, the beat of my heart.'

He looked at his dad, who was simply watching him, doing what he did best: listening while he worked his problems through. God, he was so lucky to have this man in his life. And everything he said was a fundamental truth: she was the flipside of his coin, in the best way possible. He had no idea what the future held for them, how they would—if they could—have a transcontinental relationship, how loving her would pan out.

Because it would work out; it had to. He couldn't have spent this long avoiding love to find it with a woman he didn't think he wanted it with and not have it work out.

'And are you willing to risk her leaving…?' Patrick hauled in a deep breath. 'Her dying?'

Matt made himself meet his eyes. 'Yeah. Because I

wouldn't trade those few years I had with Mom for anything and I can't live my life according to a "what if" that might never happen.'

Patrick nodded as their coffees were placed in front of them. His eyes sparkled. 'So glad we did this the easy way, over coffee, and that I didn't have to thump some sense into you.'

Matt laughed. 'I need to go back to London.'

'I figured,' Patrick said, dryly.

'Want to come? You can meet her if it works out and you can get me drunk if it doesn't.'

Patrick mulled his proposition over for about ten seconds. 'Sounds like a plan. When do we leave?'

'Poppy tells me that you won't talk to her about Matt and why he left so abruptly.'

'Jeez, give me a second to sit down first, Iz, before you take my head off,' Tori muttered as she slid into her customary seat at their favourite table in Ignite and sighed at Izzy and Poppy's grave faces. She narrowed her eyes at Poppy, who shrugged, unrepentant.

'As much as you would like to, you're not going through this alone, Toz,' Poppy firmly stated.

'And we're not going to let you pass this off as a joke or another of your bad-luck-with-men funny stories. He's too important for that,' Izzy added, glancing up at Marco, who was approaching their table. After greeting their friend, they quickly ordered and Izzy leaned forward, placing her elbows on the table.

She cocked her head as she looked at Tori. 'So, spill. What happened?'

Tori fiddled with her cutlery, pushed her hair behind her ears and thought about lying, thought about trying to put a small spin on the story. Except that she couldn't, wouldn't… He was too important to make it less than it was.

Which was terrifying.

'How are you feeling, Tori?' Poppy asked gently while she gave Izzy a not-so-subtle dig into her ribs with her elbow.

'Hollow,' Tori admitted. 'Sad. Lonely. Scared.'

'What happened?' Poppy asked. 'I heard you talking on the stairs, and then I went down to the boxroom and I could hear you crying. You wouldn't talk to me, not then, not on any of the ten times I've tried since.'

Tori heard the hurt in Poppy's voice and felt the new scratch on her soul. She never wanted to hurt anyone, not Matt, not Poppy, not herself. Izzy leaned across the table, grabbed her wrist and squeezed. 'Tori! Talk! Now!'

Tori tried, for one last time, to resist but then her tears started to fall. Poppy, ever practical, pulled out a packet of tissues from her bag, handed them over as the words tumbled out of her.

'I called it quits.'

Poppy and Izzy exchanged a long, long look before they both, at nearly the same time, screeched, *'You did what?'*

'You never call it quits. Ever. You hang on and then you hang on some more!' Izzy loudly stated. 'Why?'

'Because I need more than he can give me. Because I want love, and respect and hope for the future. Because he likes me but not enough for him to risk his heart or change his life,' Tori replied, her voice pancake flat. 'Because I love him. I had to say goodbye now before my heart is totally macerated by him.'

Izzy and Poppy stared at her as if they were seeing her for the first time. 'You love him?' Poppy asked eventually, placing her hand on Tori's. 'Properly?'

'Properly, intensely, absolutely.'

Their coffee arrived and the three friends were silent while Marco placed their cups and croissants on the table in front of them. He looked at Tori and sighed. 'Ah, *bella*.

The love, she is...how do you say in English? Kicking your butt?'

Tori couldn't help the small smile at his accurate description. 'So kicking my butt, Marco.'

Marco squeezed her shoulder before walking away and Tori took a sip of her coffee. She knew that Ignite's coffee was super delicious but, like everything else she put in her mouth, it was utterly tasteless. And the thought of eating a croissant made her stomach roil. Heartbreak was a hell of a diet plan, she decided.

'Did you tell him?' Izzy asked as she buttered her croissant, slathered it in home-made strawberry jam and popped a piece of it into her mouth.

'No,' Tori admitted.

'Why not?'

'Because I know he doesn't love me back.'

'And you know this how?' Izzy was doing her best imitation of the Grand Inquisitor and Tori squirmed in her seat. 'Did he tell you that?'

'No, I just assumed that he didn't. When I called it quits, he didn't exactly tell me he did.'

'Cos that's what guys do, Toz. They tell you that they love you after you've kicked them into touch.' Poppy lightly slapped her hand. 'How can you have dated so much but be so utterly clueless?'

'Beats me.' Izzy shrugged before speaking again. 'This isn't about Matt and the way he feels, it's about you and your scaredey-cat attitude to love.'

Tori looked at Poppy for some moral support but Poppy just leaned back in her chair, her body language screaming that she agreed with Izzy. Damn. No support from that quarter, then.

'I told you a couple of weeks ago, very intuitively, I might add, when you came across a normal man, you were going to run.'

'That's not what you said…' Tori protested.

Izzy waved her objections away. 'Close enough. What are you doing?'

Tori felt the words deep in her soul. 'Running,' she quietly admitted. 'I'm running.'

'Damn right,' Izzy stated. 'You're trying to find any excuse you can not to risk your heart because it's been so beaten up before.'

'I really didn't make good men choices before Matt,' Tori agreed.

Poppy leaned forward and shook her head. 'Please, none of those guys touched your heart. Izzy is talking about your parents, about the love and acceptance you never felt from them. They broke your heart when you were a child and you've been too scared to risk it ever since. Matt is the first person, the only man, who has ever come close enough to do any real damage.'

Tori bit her lip as Poppy continued. 'Your childhood, all of our childhoods are over, Toz. Let yourself love him, allow him the opportunity to tell you that he loves you. Don't make the assumption that he doesn't. If he doesn't, move on. If he does, great. Maybe it won't last for ever. I really hope it will, but it might not. But love is too precious a gift to throw it away.'

Even though she was in the midst of an emotional storm, Tori still heard the wistfulness in Poppy's voice, the thread of sadness. 'Take a chance, Toz. He's worth it. He's worth rolling the dice for.'

Tori gnawed on the inside of her lip and looked out of the window to the busy road. Could she? Should she? Was she brave enough? Did she really want to live with this Matt-sized crater in her heart for the rest of her life?

'I don't know. I need to think about this,' she murmured.

'Now, after all these years of making impulsive and bad decisions over yucky men, now she wants to think?

Jeez!' Izzy complained and Tori picked up a roll and threw it at her head.

'Mees Victoria...zee food!'

The battery on Matt's phone was either dead or he was, was Tori's panicked thought six hours later when she couldn't reach Matt at all. He always, always had his mobile on but she'd reached his voicemail every time she called.

Where the hell could he be? Was he okay? Who would know? Tori stood at the window in the bedroom and looked down Lancaster Road, desperately hoping that by some minor miracle she would see Matt turning the corner and heading home.

She didn't know whether he had any other friends in London and she was considering calling Drew Manning and Maya Bennet next.

She was that desperate.

The mobile in her hand chirruped and Tori nearly dropped it in excitement. Except that it wasn't Matt calling, but Isaac. *Isaac!*

'Poppy sent me a text message, telling me that you can't raise Matt,' Isaac said without preamble.

'Isaac! Do you know where he is? I should've thought about calling you! I'm such an idiot!'

'You are, especially since you kicked Matt into touch,' Isaac drawled.

Tori winced. 'I know, I know! I'm stupid but...but do you know where he is?'

Isaac took his time in replying, probably to punish her for dumping his friend. 'Why do you want to know, Tori?'

Tori closed her eyes in frustration. 'I'm in love with him and I made a mistake by shoving him away. I want to see if we can, somehow, make this work.'

'This isn't another of your whims, Victoria?'

'Promise, Isaac. He's...' Tori's voice choked up. 'I'm

crazy about him. I just need to say sorry, try and work this out.'

'That's going to be a bit difficult, honey.'

'Why?' Tori wailed.

'Mostly because he flew to Cape Town the day after you split.'

Tori took a deep breath, cursed silently and straightened her spine. 'Okay, then.'

'You're going to give up?' Isaac asked, his tone dripping with disappointment.

'Hell no! I'm going to do an Izzy and, like her, get on the first flight south.' Tori slapped her hand against the glass and spoke again, almost as if she were speaking to herself. 'I'll put in for some leave, go to Cape Town and see what's what. But how will I find him in Cape Town?'

'I know where he lives.' Isaac's low laugh rumbled into her ear. 'I'll send you all of his South African contact numbers and addresses.'

Tori let out a long, relieved sigh. 'Thanks, Isaac. Are you going to tell him that I'm on my way?'

'Do you want me to?'

Tori bit her lip. 'Not sure. Maybe I should just surprise him.'

'That's a hell of a surprise, Tori.' Isaac chuckled. 'Good luck. Oh, and remind Poppy that I'll be back soon.'

'Will do.' Tori said her goodbyes and thought that it was almost a pity that she wouldn't be around to see how Isaac and Poppy dealt with each other...all alone in this flat.

How she'd love to be a fly on the wall watching those two dance around each other. God help them. But she had her own love life to sort out, her own relationship to mend.

Eeep.

Tori manhandled her suitcase out of the boxroom and thought that she had to do something about finding somewhere else to live. Apart from the fact that living in that rabbit hutch was getting old, every time she turned around she saw Matt: in the kitchen, in the living room, sitting on the steps to the turret room.

Dammit he looked so real, so solid that she hauled in a breath and decided that she was definitely losing it. Shaking her head, she quickly ran over her mental list of what she needed. Passport, obviously, money, sun block. She looked down at her carry-on case; she could buy some summer clothes there if she was staying. If she wasn't, she'd catch the first flight home and she wouldn't need much more than the extra set of underwear, jeans and T-shirts.

'Going somewhere, Stripes?'

Tori closed her eyes as his voice slid over her, as deep as the night and as warm as honey. When she opened them again, Matt still sat on the stairs, elbows on the knees of his tired jeans, his hair messy and his jaw dark with stubble.

Matt. Dear God…

Tori just stared at him, blinked and blinked again, not entirely sure that she wasn't hallucinating. This could just be another figment of her imagination; she'd kept seeing glimpses of Matt before this—the cock of a dark head, the flash of his long, muscular legs—and her heart would lift in hope only to be slammed to the floor when she realised that the man wasn't Matt.

'Tori?'

It was him. Really him. She recognised those jeans, those flat-heeled boots, the faded T-shirt.

'What are you doing here?' she croaked, putting her hand against the wall, partly to keep herself from falling at his feet but mostly to keep from belting over to him and throwing her body into his arms.

Matt twisted his lips. 'I thought we should talk. Properly this time.'

Now or never, Victoria. Just say it. Get it out and get it done. She sent him a wobbly smile. 'Unless you're here to tell me that you love me and that you can't live without me then just walk on out of here, Matt.'

Matt's smile was wickedly amused. 'Okay, then. I'm back to tell you that I love you and that I hate living without you. Have no intention of living without you.'

'That's not funny, Matt.'

Matt stood up and jammed his hands into the pockets of his jeans. 'I never said that I was joking.'

Tori felt her heart stop. 'Wha—at?'

'You lost your hearing in the few days we've been apart, darling?'

Tori tipped her head as she allowed her bag to drop to the floor. Her eyes widened as he reached the bottom of the step and stayed there. 'Okay, let me say it louder. I love you and I miss you and I despise being apart from you.'

Matt stalked towards her and Tori couldn't take her eyes off his beautiful, tired face. Just before he reached her he stopped, faltered and looked at her again. Tori couldn't bear the hesitation on his face for one minute longer and she dashed towards him, flinging herself at him. Matt caught her as she jumped and her legs wrapped around his waist as she slammed her mouth onto his.

Home, she thought as his tongue slid past her teeth, as his fingers dug into her hips. Home. This was it. Matt's arms were the place she'd spent her whole life wanting to be. Here she felt cherished and secure and loved. So loved.

Matt whirled around, pushed her up against the wall and caught her face between the hard palms of his hands. He stared into her face, love and bewilderment and happiness replacing the exhaustion and shadows in his eyes. 'Love you, baby.'

Tori rested her forehead on his. 'Love you more. I can't believe you are here. How long are you here for?'

Matt shrugged. 'I have no damn idea. I wasn't thinking of much beyond seeing you. Holding you, having you back.'

'Thank you...' Tori bit her lip. 'Thank you for coming back. I've missed you so much...'

Matt's mouth covered hers and he kissed her and Tori sighed at the emotion she could taste, feel, in the sense of security that enveloped her. She could taste it all: the love, acceptance, support, lust, passion...laughter. All the things she'd so desperately wished for, wanted.

All wrapped up in this hard-bodied, green-eyed man who said he loved her.

Tori slid down his body, grabbed his hand and led him back to the stairs. Matt sat down and Tori snuggled up into his body. 'I was on my way to see you.'

Matt pulled back, frowning. 'What?'

Tori reached behind her and pulled her passport and ticket out of the back pocket of her jeans. 'I was coming to you. To tell you that I was miserable without you. That I love you and to ask whether we could give it another shot. I was, obviously, fully expecting you to say no but I didn't want to regret not asking.'

Matt kissed her head and Tori didn't see him closing his eyes in relief. 'Thanks. I needed that.' He pulled back and looked down at her, relief and satisfaction and happiness burning in his eyes. 'What about work? Did you take some holiday time?'

Tori shrugged, her hands gripping his hips. 'I told them that I was burning out, that I needed some time away. Judging by the fact that I have been less than useless for the last two weeks, I think my bosses believed me and they've given me all the time I'm owed. Somewhere around three weeks, I think.'

Matt rested his forehead on hers. 'Well, since you have a ticket, fly back to SA with us.'

Tori lifted her eyebrows. 'Us?'

Matt looked embarrassed. 'My dad flew over with me, to meet you if it worked out. To support me if it didn't.'

Tori smiled, touched. 'I can't wait to meet him and, yes, I'd love to go to Cape Town with you.'

'And then? After the three weeks.' Matt stroked her cheekbone with his thumb. 'What do we do then?'

Tori rested her forehead against his collarbone. 'I've been thinking about that too. While I was fully convinced that there was no way you could love me—'

'Which I do, more than you will ever know,' Matt interrupted her.

Tori's smile wobbled with emotion. 'Well, I couldn't help but dream a little. So, I was thinking that if you wanted me around, like full-time—'

'Only as much as I want to keep breathing,' Matt assured her.

'Okay, that's a good start. So I'm presuming that, with opening a new branch of your business in London, you might be spending a bit more time in London than you were before?'

'That was the plan. Three months here, three there. I was thinking of finding a flat here.'

Tori touched her fingers to his cheek and kept them there. 'Good. Well, *I was thinking* that I could maybe do some freelance work, offer my services to PR companies for special projects, both here and in Cape Town. BB&K have a branch there. That way I could be with you here and there—we could be together. If that's what you want.'

'That's what I need, sweetheart.' Matt brushed the hair back from her face, his eyes blazing with love...for her. 'But will you be happy, doing that? Two homes, two countries? I'll move to London full time if that would make you happier. I just want you to be happy. And on that point, I know that I need to make some changes, find some balance between work and my personal life. Start giving my clients some boundaries. Because, while they are important, nobody is more important than you. Ever. They are my bread and butter, sometimes my jam, but you, Victoria… you are—for me—the reason the sun rises every morning.'

Tori blinked away the moisture in her eyes. 'God, Matt, you kill me. You say all the right things. But your business and your dad need you in Cape Town and I need to be with you so let's try the living in two countries thing for now.'

Tori felt his mouth settle over hers and she sighed. This was where she was meant to be, she realised. In Cape Town, in a flat here in London, in love with Matt. This was her definition of happiness. Of home. Of love.

Tori's lips nuzzled his jaw. She'd found it, Tori thought. A love as deep as the Mariana trench, someone who would say I love you every night and who would prove it every day.

'I'm so damn happy,' Matt whispered before he kissed her, his lips and mouth and tongue filling her with emotion, security and sheer joy.

'Good,' she whispered back. 'Me too. How about taking me to meet your dad, Matt? Isaac said that I'd like him.'

'You will and I will take you to meet him. But later… much, much later. Like hours and hours from now. I have plans for you right now.' Matt's hand lifted up and covered her breast, his fingers finding her nipple as his tongue slid into her mouth. Passion rose in a white-hot wave and suddenly they were tearing at each other's clothes, frantic to be skin on skin.

They didn't hear the front door opening, nor did they hear two sets of feet clomping their way towards them. When Isaac's deep voice finally broke through their sexual haze, Tori was down to her bra and Matt was shirtless.

'Dear God, on the stairs?' Poppy demanded and Isaac laughed. 'That can't be comfortable.'

Matt tossed Tori her shirt but she just held it in her hand, too happy to feel embarrassed. 'Put your shirt on, Stripes.'

Isaac grinned. 'Don't bother on my account—I'm a huge fan of sexy lingerie. Especially green lingerie.'

'It's lemon sherbet, not green,' Tori corrected him as she lay back on the stairs, utterly relaxed. She sent Poppy a huge grin. 'Matt's back.'

Poppy's mouth twitched. 'I see that. I'm glad.'

'He loves me.' Tori sent Matt a goofy grin.

'I'd love you even more if you'd—please!—put that shirt on, darling,' Matt begged.

Poppy didn't lift her eyes off Tori's beaming face. 'I can see that too. I'm happy for you, darling,' Poppy said, her tone gentle. 'But why don't you take him to your room?'

Tori sighed and stood up. 'The stairs are way more comfortable than the bed in the boxroom.'

Poppy blushed. 'Tori Phillips, you are not doing it on my stairs! Ever!'

Tori grinned as she held out a hand to Matt as Poppy and Isaac passed them on the stairs. On the way to the boxroom, they heard Isaac's amused voice. 'Judging by the look on their faces, I guess they've been there, done that, got the carpet burns. I might just have to try it myself.'

'Do it and die,' Poppy snapped.

In the crowded boxroom Tori whirled into Matt's arms, smiling widely. 'A part of me wants to stay here and watch how Poppy deals with Isaac, but all of me just wants to spend three weeks, the rest of my life, in a massive bed with you.'

'Yep, something is sparking between them but, right now, I don't care. You and I, on the other hand…' Matt placed his arms under her butt and lifted her up and into him. Tori's legs wrapped around his waist and she lowered her forehead to his.

Tori's lips quirked. 'You and I…what?'

Matt just looked at her for a long, long moment. 'Just…
you. And me. *For* me. This is it.'

He lowered her to the tiny bed, keeping his eyes on
her face as he followed her down, placing his knees on
either side of hers, capturing her face in his hands. 'God,
I love—'

A loud, creaking sound interrupted his Romeo moment
and he looked at Tori in horror. She just started to giggle.

'Um, Stripes, I think the bed is about to collapse,' Matt
muttered, pulling back.

Tori looped her arms around his neck and pulled him
down for a long, wet kiss. 'Let it. It can do whatever it
wants as long as you keep kissing me, loving me…'

'That I can do…'

Craaaccccckkkkk.

As quick as a whip, Matt rolled her over so that she was
on top and his eyes sparkled with mirth.

The movement caused the bed to moan again.
Crrrrrrrrraaaaaaaaccckkkkkkkk.

'Oh, hell…here we go.' Matt's arms tightened around
her. 'I've got you, babe.'

Tori just laughed as the mattress fell out of the now broken frame and headed to the floor with them following in
a tangled heap. 'Oh, Matt, you really do.'

* * * * *

If you loved this book, make sure you catch
the rest of the incredible
THE FLAT IN NOTTING HILL *miniseries!*

THE MORNING AFTER THE NIGHT BEFORE
by Nikki Logan
available August 2014

SLEEPING WITH THE SOLDIER
by Charlotte Phillips
available September 2014

ENEMIES WITH BENEFITS
by Louisa George
available November 2014

Mills & Boon® Hardback
October 2014

ROMANCE

An Heiress for His Empire	Lucy Monroe
His for a Price	Caitlin Crews
Commanded by the Sheikh	Kate Hewitt
The Valquez Bride	Melanie Milburne
The Uncompromising Italian	Cathy Williams
Prince Hafiz's Only Vice	Susanna Carr
A Deal Before the Altar	Rachael Thomas
Rival's Challenge	Abby Green
The Party Starts at Midnight	Lucy King
Your Bed or Mine?	Joss Wood
Turning the Good Girl Bad	Avril Tremayne
Breaking the Bro Code	Stefanie London
The Billionaire in Disguise	Soraya Lane
The Unexpected Honeymoon	Barbara Wallace
A Princess by Christmas	Jennifer Faye
His Reluctant Cinderella	Jessica Gilmore
One More Night with Her Desert Prince...	Jennifer Taylor
From Fling to Forever	Avril Tremayne

MEDICAL

It Started with No Strings...	Kate Hardy
Flirting with Dr Off-Limits	Robin Gianna
Dare She Date Again?	Amy Ruttan
The Surgeon's Christmas Wish	Annie O'Neil

Mills & Boon® Large Print

October 2014

ROMANCE

HISTORICAL

MEDICAL

ROMANCE

A Virgin for His Prize	Lucy Monroe
The Valquez Seduction	Melanie Milburne
Protecting the Desert Princess	Carol Marinelli
One Night with Morelli	Kim Lawrence
To Defy a Sheikh	Maisey Yates
The Russian's Acquisition	Dani Collins
The True King of Dahaar	Tara Pammi
Rebel's Bargain	Annie West
The Million-Dollar Question	Kimberly Lang
Enemies with Benefits	Louisa George
Man vs. Socialite	Charlotte Phillips
Fired by Her Fling	Christy McKellen
The Twelve Dates of Christmas	Susan Meier
At the Chateau for Christmas	Rebecca Winters
A Very Special Holiday Gift	Barbara Hannay
A New Year Marriage Proposal	Kate Hardy
A Little Christmas Magic	Alison Roberts
Christmas with the Maverick Millionaire	Scarlet Wilson

MEDICAL

Playing the Playboy's Sweetheart	Carol Marinelli
Unwrapping Her Italian Doc	Carol Marinelli
A Doctor by Day...	Emily Forbes
Tamed by the Renegade	Emily Forbes

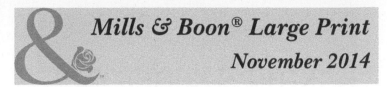

Mills & Boon® Large Print

November 2014

ROMANCE

Christakis's Rebellious Wife	Lynne Graham
At No Man's Command	Melanie Milburne
Carrying the Sheikh's Heir	Lynn Raye Harris
Bound by the Italian's Contract	Janette Kenny
Dante's Unexpected Legacy	Catherine George
A Deal with Demakis	Tara Pammi
The Ultimate Playboy	Maya Blake
Her Irresistible Protector	Michelle Douglas
The Maverick Millionaire	Alison Roberts
The Return of the Rebel	Jennifer Faye
The Tycoon and the Wedding Planner	Kandy Shepherd

HISTORICAL

A Lady of Notoriety	Diane Gaston
The Scarlet Gown	Sarah Mallory
Safe in the Earl's Arms	Liz Tyner
Betrayed, Betrothed and Bedded	Juliet Landon
Castle of the Wolf	Margaret Moore

MEDICAL

200 Harley Street: The Proud Italian	Alison Roberts
200 Harley Street: American Surgeon in London	Lynne Marshall
A Mother's Secret	Scarlet Wilson
Return of Dr Maguire	Judy Campbell
Saving His Little Miracle	Jennifer Taylor
Heatherdale's Shy Nurse	Abigail Gordon

MILLS & BOON®

Why shop at millsandboon.co.uk?

Each year, thousands of romance readers find their perfect read at millsandboon.co.uk. That's because we're passionate about bringing you the very best romantic fiction. Here are some of the advantages of shopping at www.millsandboon.co.uk:

* **Get new books first**—you'll be able to buy your favourite books one month before they hit the shops

* **Get exclusive discounts**—you'll also be able to buy our specially created monthly collections, with up to 50% off the RRP

* **Find your favourite authors**—latest news, interviews and new releases for all your favourite authors and series on our website, plus ideas for what to try next

* **Join in**—once you've bought your favourite books, don't forget to register with us to rate, review and join in the discussions

Visit **www.millsandboon.co.uk**
for all this and more today!